The Money Shot

by: D. Mann

ISBN: 978-692-05238-9

Part 1

Wild Heart

I

Duncan stood at the window looking out at the desert sunset, reds and oranges tapering to blue gray. He looked at his watch again; it was ten minutes past the last time he looked at it. He pulled the curtain shut and turned around to look at his sparse motel room done in pastel oranges and yellows. A queen-sized bed took up most of the space with a wood and steel headboard that looked like half a wagon wheel. Beside the bed was a wooden chair that looked like it might have belonged to a dinette set twenty years ago. Across from the foot of the bed hung a small flat screen TV and beneath that a chipped and scarred waist high dresser covered in cigarette burns. On the far side of the bed in the corner was a nightstand with a lamp and telephone.

Duncan walked past the foot of the bed to the bathroom door and flipped on the light. The bathtub, toilet and sink were all nearly touching and yellowed with age. The Sagebrush Inn certainly wasn't the Ritz, Duncan thought, but it was at least some place that let him pay in cash and didn't ask for ID. He looked in the mirror at himself for the umpteenth time and told himself he wasn't doing too bad for being forty-one. He still had most of his sandy brown hair that he parted on the right side since he was old enough to hold a comb. His face was clean shaven - he'd tried to grow a mustache once but thought it made him look like a pedophile, so it was quickly removed. Like most middle aged men, he had a little extra weight encircling his waist, but he could still see his dick and kept telling himself he was going to exercise, so he figured it wasn't all bad.

A knock at the door sent his heart racing. He looked at himself one final time in the mirror, hit the light off and went to the motel door. He took a deep breath, put on his accountant smile and pulled open the door.

"Hi, are you Duncan?" the tall, slender woman in the doorway asked.

With a wide shit-eating grin Duncan nodded his head and stepped aside to let her in. He tried to say something but his tongue suddenly felt too big for his mouth and he stopped himself, afraid he'd only be able to babble like an idiot. The woman walked into the motel room and in her four inch stiletto heels she was almost eye to eye with Duncan's 5'9" height. He shut the door and let his eyes drool over the new lady in his life.

She had straight, long blonde hair with dark half inch roots that was parted in the center and draped down her shoulders and back reaching to about her elbows. Her dress was like a painted on tube that hugged her body from her armpits to mid thigh. It was blue and black with white jagged lines that made Duncan think of lightning bolts in a thunderstorm. A red, green and purple tattoo of vines and flowers was above her right shoulder blade and on the back of her left thigh was a prominent six inch white scar that contrasted with her otherwise darkly tanned skin.

"Are you a cop?" the lady asked as she turned around to face him.

Duncan almost laughed thinking he was the furthest thing from a cop. "No," he said shaking his head. But then a wave of heat and fear washed over him as he recalled watching some True Crime TV program where the cops were always the first to ask this question to try to fool the bad guys.

"How do I know you're not a cop?" Duncan asked.

The lady tilted her head and raised her eyebrows in a gesture that said 'Are you kidding me?' but then she smiled. "Have a seat," she told Duncan as she moved aside and motioned toward the bed. Nervously he sat down and looked up at her. The woman stepped forward and slid the bottom of her dress up over her hips as she lifted her right leg and set it on the bed.

"Taste me," she told him.

Duncan swallowed and looked up at her face, unsure he heard her correctly.

"Go on, do it," she said. "Stick out your tongue and taste me."

Duncan looked at the pussy only inches from his face. He felt his body trembling, though he didn't know if it was fear or excitement. His mouth was dry but he still managed to lick his lips as he moved his head forward to lick her lips. Her pussy was shaved save for a small patch of dark fur just above her slit. It looked like it was in the shape of a heart, though a few of the pubes were a little longer and wilder.

Duncan's tongue touched the warm, soft skin of her vulva and he breathed in her scent of vanilla and something flowery and something sexual. His mouth watered as he licked her a second time tasting her clean, soapy skin and a hint of saltiness and sweetness. He was getting lost in her womanhood as his third lick pushed between her pussy lips like a little kid trying to get to the center of a Tootsie Pop.

He felt her hand on his head and thought for sure she was going to pull him into her but instead she pushed his head away.

"Does that taste like pork to you?" she asked looking down at him.

Duncan smiled and shook his head no.

"Okay, then," the prostitute said as she put her leg back on the floor and tugged her skirt back to her slender thighs. "But I still don't know if you're a cop of not. How do I know you're not packing heat?" she asked as she bent forward and grasped his hard cock through his beige Dockers. "Oh my," she said as she gave him a couple strokes through the fabric. "Let me see your wallet."

Duncan looked at her as if she had spoken Japanese. When he didn't comply, she stopped stroking him and squeezed his cock in her grasp. He almost thought he'd explode right there. "Your wallet, give it to me," she demanded.

Duncan reached around to his right rear pocket and pulled out a thin, brown leather wallet and handed it to her. She let go of his crotch and opened his wallet. She looked at him after examining his driver's license.

"Your last name is cock?" she asked.

"It's pronounced Coke. K-O-C-H," Duncan said.

"I can see how it's spelled. Where's Medford, Oregon?"

"A little ways past the California border," Duncan answered as he watched her looking through his wallet. His eyes kept drifting to her small pear shaped breasts and the slight protrusion of nipples he could see poking through the fabric.

"You're a long way from home."

"It was about a sixteen hour drive. But it's not home anymore."

"You drove that old car out there all that way?" she asked as she handed him his wallet back.

"That's a '66 Mustang - it's a classic."

"Hmmph," she replied, seemingly not impressed. "This is for me?" she asked as he reached for three hundred-dollar bills atop the dresser.

"Yeah. I don't need change."

"I don't give change."

"No, what I mean is that the other fifty is your tip."

"Thanks," she said and picked up a small black bag from the floor that Duncan hadn't remembered her setting down. Obviously, his eyes and attention were on other things. "I'm going to step in here and then we'll get started," the lady of the night said as she walked to the bathroom door. Duncan's mouth watered and his loins tingled as he watched her ass wiggle beneath the tight fabric of her dress.

"Oh my god!" Duncan mumbled to himself as soon as the door closed. He put his hand to his mouth and bit down on his thumb to make sure he wasn't dreaming. He wasn't sure if she was twenty-two or thirty-two, but with looks like that it didn't matter. He could still smell the fragrance of her pussy on his lips.

He stood up from the bed and had to adjust his semi-hard chub and then patted his pants to blot up the pre-cum on his inner thigh. He wondered if he should get naked and get on the bed or wait for her to come out. He'd never done anything like this before and it was both exhilarating and nerve-wracking. He decided to pull off his blue Polo shirt but leave his pants on and see where it went from there.

The water could be heard running in the bathroom as he sat back down on the edge of the bed. He kept his feet on the floor but leaned back onto his elbows, thinking he must look cool but feeling silly. He got up and decided to lean against the dresser facing the bathroom with his arms crossed. No, that didn't feel right. The water in the bathroom stopped and Duncan looked around in a panic where he should sit or stand. His cell phone on the nightstand rang and he almost screamed.

II

"Betty, you can't keep calling like this," Duncan said after grabbing the phone and walking to the foot of the bed. The bathroom door opened less than two feet away from him and the prostitute stepped out.

"Are you ready, baby?" she asked.

Duncan's eyes went wide and he immediately put his forefinger against her lips to hush her. "No, uh-uh, that was just the TV," he said into his phone.

The woman in front of him smiled mischievously, parted her lips and slowly began to suck his finger into her mouth. She was wearing a silky, sheer white robe that barely reached to her waist and he could see the dark pink patches of her nipples and areola through the fabric. The small robe was untied and Duncan could see the curve of one of her breasts

5

through the opening and it reminded him of a ski jump he'd seen on the winter Olympics. She popped the wet finger from between her lips and then went down to her knees in front of him.

"All the begging and pleading in the world isn't going to change anything," Duncan said, his voice wavering slightly. He looked down to see the woman's head at waist high, her one hand on his belt and her other hand pulling down his zipper.

"I told you, I had to get out of there," he said with the phone beside his face. The woman before him reached into his fly and pulled him out. His hard cock sprang to attention like a flag on the Fourth of July.

"I know it's hard," he said and then listened but paying more attention to the lady's small, hot hands wrapping around his shaft. She looked up at him through her long lashes and for the first time Duncan took in her blue green eyes that were like warm, Caribbean waters. She opened her red painted mouth and slipped it over the head of his cock.

"Yeah, it sucks. It really, really sucks," he mumbled into the phone as hands and mouth slid up and down the length of his throbbing cock. Duncan closed his eyes and moaned lightly. "No, I didn't say anything," he said, finding it almost impossible to pay attention to the person on the other end of the line. He was lost in the sensations of lip sucking, tongue swirling, hand stroking action. When her other hand slipped underneath him to fondle and pull on his balls, he knew he was about to lose it.

"Listen, I gotta go," he said quickly. "No, bye. I gotta go." Duncan disconnected the call and dropped the phone on the bed. "Oh god, I'm gonna go," he groaned as his legs quivered and his ass convulsed. He braced himself against the wall with one hand while his other hand went to the back of her head. His cock fired off like a water cannon and he grunted loudly as she stroked and milked him expertly.

She pulled her head back and his cock flopped out of her mouth. He was surprised to see that his dick was wrapped in an ultra thin condom that she had slipped on him using only her mouth.

"How was that?" she asked, looking up at him from her knees.

"How was that?" Betty asked as she looked up at the man with the dreadlocks standing beside her in the dinette area of her small townhome. She was a mousy school teacher about thirty pounds overweight with her dark brown hair in a tight bun. Her baggy gray sweater and brown pants all but hid her figure.

Croak, as the man in the dreads was known, had been standing beside her motionless as he listened to the phone call on her speaker phone. He was tall, slender and had a pale white face that looked like it had been chiseled from granite with a dull tool. He wore a poncho that looked like it had been stolen from the set of a '70's era Clint Eastwood western. Croak looked at Betty and then across the table to his partner BC.

BC was big, bulky and black and he made the dinette table look like it was a child's toy. He was bent over a computer tablet on the table, his bald dome reflecting the overhead lights as his beefy fingers typed away on the little screen. He looked up at Croak and smiled, flashing his gold, diamond encrusted tooth.

"We pinged him," BC said, his voice deep and echoing like it came from within a cave. "Thirty miles outside of Vegas."

"Vegas!" Betty exclaimed. "Las Vegas? What's he doing there? Duncan doesn't even like to gamble. Why would he--"

Betty's mouth stopped working when she saw Croak's poncho raise and in his hand was a scary looking chrome revolver with a hole at the end of the barrel big enough to put her thumb into.

"How long until we can be there?" Croak asked, his voice ice cold.

"We're on a flight in the morning, already booked," BC told him as he got up from the table.

Croak held the .44 Magnum on Betty and he looked from BC to Betty with no sign of emotion or intent.

"Ma'am," BC said in an almost soothing, gentle tone that sent a shiver down her spine. What he said next caused her to piss herself. "If you attempt to contact your fiancée we will be forced to come back and hurt you."

IV

"I don't want to hurt you," Duncan panted.

"Harder! Fuck me harder!" the prostitute cried. "Yes! There, right there. Yes!"

She was on her hands and knees in the middle of the bed and Duncan was up on his knees behind her, his cock jack hammering into her pussy from behind, their bodies slapping together loudly. His hands were clasped to her hips and he pulled her into him with each thrust forward.

The woman grabbed one of the pillows from near the wagon wheel headboard and she buried her head into it. Duncan looked down the slope of her long, slender back and tilted his head to see one of her tits bouncing against the mattress as he pounded her harder.

"Oh god," Duncan moaned.

"No!" she said. "Don't you go yet. I'm almost there. Harder!"

Sweat beaded on his brow as he gave it all he had. Her pussy was tight and without question the best he ever had and this experience was worth every dollar, but he took a little offense to the fact she was telling him what do for her pleasure. He thought this was supposed to be all about him and his pleasure.

Of course he had certainly been pleased with the blowjob thirty minutes ago and after he'd dumped the condom in the toilet he returned to find her bent over pulling the bedspread from the mattress. He stood mesmerized with her perfectly heart shaped ass and had a moment's remorse that he'd blown his load so quickly.

"What's the matter?" she asked when she turned and saw the look on his face.

Duncan shook his head and said, "It's all good." He smiled and painted her body up and down with his eyes. She smiled and looked at his limp dick.

"Don't worry," she said, "we have plenty of time to bring him back to life. Come here."

She scooted herself onto the bed by the pillows and patted the mattress. Like a puppy dog he obeyed and moved beside her, propping himself up on an elbow and facing her.

"I hope I didn't ruin your phone call," she said with a sly smile. "So, what, you have a wife or girlfriend or something?"

"Fiancée," Duncan answered. "Well, ex-fiancée."

"Hmm, does she know she's an ex?"

"I think I've made it clear."

"What's wrong, you don't want to be married, or you just don't want to be married to her?"

"Betty's a good girl but I realized I needed something different."

"So you came to Vegas for something different?"

Duncan smiled. "This is definitely something different." He looked at her body leaning against the headboard. She still wore the white robe but it hung uselessly at her sides exposing both breasts. Her legs were crossed and he focused on the furry little heart. He reached out with a finger and traced it around the heart. "I came across a once-in-a-lifetime opportunity and decided it was now or never. I'm not getting any younger."

"A lot of guys come to Vegas in a midlife crisis."

"I'm on my way to Miami," he told her. "I'm not even going to the strip. I don't gamble."

"Life is a gamble," she said. "I heard somewhere once that you should try your luck every day because otherwise you could be going around lucky all day and not even know it."

"I like that."

"I like that," she cooed. Duncan's finger had been joined by another and they had meandered from petting the heart pubes to now sliding up and down the slit of her pussy. She leaned back and uncrossed her legs, spreading them out on the bed, one of them brushing up against Duncan's thigh. He looked at her beautiful face and watched her tongue slide across her lips. He licked his own lips and moved toward her.

She turned her head slightly away. "I don't kiss. It's too intimate."

"Oh," he said feeling dejected.

She turned back to him and kissed his cheek and then sucked on his earlobe. "But you can do anything else to me that you want."

"Anything?"

"Anything," she whispered, her breath hot in his ear.

He slipped his fingers into her as he kissed her neck and shoulder and then wrapped his mouth around a nipple and breast. She moaned lightly and Duncan could feel himself coming to life as he fingered her and sucked on her succulent titty. Twenty minutes later he had sweat dripping onto her ass as he jerked his hips back and forth for all he was worth.

"Oh fuck! Yes! Fuckfuckfuck!" she screamed out as she grabbed two spokes of the headboard and rattled the bed as orgasms rattled her body.

"Auughh!" Duncan roared as his cock exploded like a pent up volcano and he ground his pelvis hard against her ass cheeks. Small aftershocks spasmed through both their bodies as he draped his sweaty body over her back.

V

"Oh that was good," the prostitute mumbled, her face still smooshed into the pillow.

"The best," Duncan said. He pulled out of her and rolled beside her on the bed before his burning thighs gave out on him. His jizz-filled condom flopped against his thigh. The wonderful woman beside him lay on her back and draped an arm across his chest. "Can I ask you something?" he asked.

"Sure."

"What's your name?"

"Well aren't you the charmer," she laughed. "Just kidding. I'm Fantasia."

"Your parents named you after a Mickey Mouse cartoon?"

She laughed again. Duncan liked her laugh. Betty never laughed enough, he thought.

"I named me," she told him.

"So that's not your real name?"

"This isn't real."

"It sure felt real to me," Duncan said.

"I'm glad I pleased you. I liked it too. But it's all just a fantasy. In about ten minutes I'll walk out the door and you'll never see me again."

"But what if I called you again?"

"I thought you were going to Miami?"

"I am."

Fantasia sat up on the bed and grabbed his wilted member in one hand and slipped the condom off him. She carried it to the bathroom and he heard the toilet flush. The water in the sink came on. "I had a good time," she said from the bathroom.

"Why do you do it?" Duncan asked, sitting up on the bed now.

"Do what?"

"This job. Is it just about the money?"

He could hear splashing water and he imagined her rinsing her face and dabbing parts of her naked body. "When I was a little girl my grandma told me to do what you love and find a way to get paid doing it. I love to fuck. And the money's nice."

"Was your grandma a prostitute?"

Fantasia's sing-song laugh filled the room again. "No, grandma worked in a department store until her dying day, never really happy and never having any money."

"What if you never had to worry about money? What if you could get away from all this?"

The water stopped and she stepped halfway out of the bathroom to look at Duncan with a bemused look. His eyes rolled down her breast with its perky, pink nipple and over the curve of her hip and down her long leg to her toe tips painted midnight rose. "Are you offering me the Richard Gere, Pretty Woman escape dream?"

"What if I am?"

Fantasia laughed. Duncan smiled, loving to see her happy.

"You're in a fifty dollar motel room and driving a fifty year old car," she pointed out with no malice in her tone. "Usually the guys that are trying to rescue me have suites at Caesars's Palace or the MGM and offering to buy me a pair of twenty-five hundred dollar Jimmy Choo's."

"Is that what you want, some Jimmy shoes?"

"Jimmy Choo's," she smiled. "I'm happy with my life."

"But what if I could make you happier?"

Now her smile had a tinge of sadness to it. "I have to go," she said and turned back to the bathroom.

"Get dressed," Duncan said. "I want to show you something."

"Duncan."

"Please? Just humor me."

Five minutes later Duncan was wearing his Dockers and Fantasia was squeezed into her tube dress and they were standing in the dark parking lot behind Duncan's Mustang. A lone yellow street light cast a glow from thirty feet away. Using the key, Duncan opened the trunk and then bent inside and opened a large leather bag. He stood up, looked at Fantasia and smiled.

She looked into the trunk and then back at Duncan. "What? It's too dark, I can't see anything."

Duncan reached into the trunk and lifted the bag out and balanced it on the bumper. He angled the opening to catch the street light and Fantasia looked inside.

"Is that...money?"

"Over eight hundred thousand dollars," Duncan said proudly. "More than enough for a whole new life in Miami. Even for two."

Fantasia put her hand on Duncan's shoulder and gave it a light squeeze. "I'm happy with my life here," she told him.

Slowly he set the bag back into the trunk. He was about to close the trunk but stopped. "What about for tonight?" he asked her.

"What about it?"

"How much for you to stay the night with me?"

She looked at him in the dark parking lot, half his face aglow in the yellow street light. "That might not be a good idea," she said. "I'm not going to change my mind if that's what you think."

"That's not what I'm thinking," he said shaking his head. "I'm thinking you said you like to fuck and I want to fuck and keep fucking until I get the fuck out of town. How much?"

Fantasia looked at him and then into the dark trunk, considering.

"I just want to have fun," Duncan told her.

She looked at him and smiled. "How much fun? I could call a girlfriend to come play with us."

"Sounds like we're having us a party," he replied and grabbed some of the money out of the bag before shutting the trunk.

They returned to the motel room and Fantasia made the call, hoping that having another girl present would lighten up his emotional attachment. "What do you like to drink?" she asked Duncan. "I'm having her pick up a pizza, too."

VI

A little over an hour later and after a little play time in the shower, Duncan and Fantasia were lounging naked on the bed, their damp towels in heaps on the floor. There was knock at the door and Fantasia jumped off the bed with an excited squeal of a teenager. Duncan smiled as he watched her open the door with no thought to her nakedness.

"What's up, bitches!" the cute little Asian said on the other side of the door. She was maybe 5'2" and a hundred pounds with obviously fake big titties stuffed in a neon lime green tank top. She held a pizza box in her hands and had a large, pink Victoria's Secret bag hanging from her shoulder that seemed almost half as big as she was.

"Kiki!" Fantasia exclaimed. "Come in, come in."

"Well hello," Kiki said, looking at Duncan's naked body kicked back on the bed. She looked at Fantasia and asked, "Is this desert?"

"That's Duncan. Duncan, this is Kiki," Fantasia said as she took the pizza box and set it on the dresser. The smiling Asian lady slipped the pink bag from her shoulder and approached the bed.

"Hi," Duncan said and stuck out his hand.

Kiki avoided it and instead grabbed his limp dick and gave it a shake. "Nice to meet you. What are we going to do about this?"

Fantasia laughed and said, "That's why we needed pizza to reenergize."

"I see," she replied and gave him another squeeze before letting his dick go. "I've got just the thing."

Duncan smiled at Fantasia who shrugged her shoulders as Kiki went to her bag. "Here," she said to her girlfriend, handing her items from the bag: a bottle of Captain Morgan, a two-liter bottle of Coke, a double headed dildo. "Oops, that's for later," she said and put it back in the bag. "Ah, here it is," she said as she pulled out a small prescription bottle. She shook out a blue pill and handed it to Duncan.

"What's this?" he asked, though pretty certain he already knew the answer.

"That will put little Duncan back into the game," Kiki said with a smile. Fantasia was pouring together the Captain and Cokes in small plastic motel cups.

"I don't think--" Duncan began to say but Kiki cut him off.

"Just do it! As Nike says," and she handed him one of the cups. He looked to Fantasia who nodded and smiled and then he just did it.

"I'm way too over-dressed for this party," Kiki said and seconds later her clothes were on the floor. Duncan checked her out from her black and red streaked hair that almost reached her shoulders to her breasts that seemed almost too big for her little body to a waist so small he thought he might be able to wrap his two hands around it and have all his fingers touch. She had a shaved pussy that glittered from a couple piercings but his attention kept being drawn to her breasts and the smallest nipples he'd ever seen in his life that looked like watermelon seeds. Her boobs reminded him of two large cartoon eyeballs popping out of someone's head when frightened or excited.

"I take it you approve?" Fantasia said as she handed him a slice of pepperoni pizza. Duncan sat on the edge of the bed, pizza in one hand and drink in the other, and nodded appreciatively.

"Do you mind if I have a seat?" Kiki asked. Before Duncan could respond or realize what was happening, she was nuzzling her ass in his lap, a piece of pizza and drink in her hands.

Fantasia laughed and said, "Kiki can be a little much."

"You're just mad because I took your seat," Kiki said and stuck out her tongue.

Fantasia returned the gesture and said, "I've already sat there."

"Touché," the Asian replied. "Don't worry, girlfriend, I'll give you a place to sit in a little bit." She finished her pizza slice and then slipped her hand between her legs to feel Duncan beneath her. "I don't know if it's the pizza or the pill, but something's working."

Duncan blushed and Fantasia giggled. Kiki lifted her hips and with her free hand positioned his hardening cock and then slid her pussy atop him. For a brief second, he thought he should say something about putting on a condom but then all cohesive thought was lost as he felt something he'd never experienced in his life. Kiki's body didn't move atop him but the muscles in her pussy flexed and squeezed and worked like miniature hands stroking him up and down inside her.

"Oh man, you should see the look on his face," Fantasia said as she reached for another piece of pizza. She offered one to Kiki but she shook her head and took a sip of her drink. Duncan looked as if he was in a trance, his drink and pizza almost falling from his hands. "I've been practicing that move but still haven't gotten it down."

"Come here," Kiki told her and when she did Kiki licked her four little fingers and then slipped them up Fantasia's pussy. "Let me feel. Are you doing it? Oh wait, there, I can feel it a little. You've got to do more of those Kiegel exercises I showed you." Kiki pulled her fingers out and stuck them in her mouth.

"I've been trying," Fantasia said and then stifled a yawn.

"Oh no you didn't!" Kiki exclaimed and jumped out of Duncan's lap, leaving his boner bouncing in his lap.

VII

"What did I do?" Duncan asked, a shocked look on his face.

"Not you, her," Kiki said and then looked at Duncan. "And you, too! You both look like you're ready to lie down and go to sleep." She dug around in her large pink bag and produced a small, red plastic container. "I was promised a party, so I'm going to make it a party," she said as she sat on

16

the edge of the bed next to Duncan. She opened the red container and proceeded to pour a little white line of powder atop her right breast and an identical line on her left breast. "Who's first?"

Duncan looked from the powdery line to Fantasia and before he could say anything she stepped forward, bent down and snorted the line from Kiki's left tit. What the fuck, Duncan thought, when in Rome.... He leaned over and snorted the white line off her right tit. Within seconds he felt like a neon sign that had been plugged in and turned on and was now humming with energy.

"Stand up, big boy," Kiki told him. "Now stand still." She tapped out a line of powder atop his rigid cock and then she leaned forward and snorted it off. She tapped out another line on his member and told Fantasia, "This one's for your other nostril, girlfriend!"

Fantasia got on her knees and snorted up the second line.

"Did you get it all?" Kiki asked.

"I don't know. We better make sure," Fantasia said and ran her tongue along the ridge of his cock. Kiki got on her knees and began following suit, sliding her tongue back and forth the length of his shaft. Duncan put his hands on his ass and arched his back, soaking in the sensation as he watched the two mouths and lips and tongues moving back and forth and at times touching and licking each other. He moaned pleasantly as Kiki's small lips wrapped around the tip of his cock and Fantasia's mouth disappeared between his legs and began sucking on his balls. Kiki's head began bobbing, slowly at first and then more vigorously and he could feel the sucking and tugging of his testicles and the fire within him began to roar and surge and just before his dam busted loose Kiki pulled him from her pretty mouth and her hands stroked him wildly and his cum spurted out onto her face, her chin, her breasts.

"Oh fuck yeah," Kiki cried out as she squeezed and milked his cock and stuck out her tongue to catch the last

17

sticky drops and then sucked his tip for any last remaining goodness.

"Kiki's got a little cum fetish," Fantasia said as Duncan watched the Asian smear his man juice on her tits and face and then licked her hands clean.

"Duncan and I need to hit our other nostrils," Kiki declared. To Fantasia she said, "Up on the bed, girlfriend."

"Oh, I'm okay," Duncan said, felling plenty buzzed.

"I know you're okay. This will make you great!" Kiki said.

Duncan was about to decline until Fantasia got on her knees on the bed and bent down, her ass facing him and Kiki. Kiki poured a line of powder in the crack of her friend's ass and looked at Duncan. "You're up!"

Duncan placed his hands on Fantasia's ass, spread the cheeks slightly, and snorted up the line like he was a Hoover vacuum cleaner. He felt like he'd been zapped by lightning. Kiki replaced another line in Fantasia's ass crack, snorted it up and then ran her tongue up and down the crack for good measure.

"Okay kids, let's play!" Kiki said as she went to her pink bag and pulled it to the edge of the bed on the floor. Duncan and Fantasia looked at each other and laughed at the Asian's enthusiasm. "Here we go!" she said and pulled out two pairs of pink handcuffs. "I'm first!"

Kiki's wrists were handcuffed spread eagle to the spokes of the wagon wheel headboard and Duncan was on his knees between her legs, his cock sliding in and out of her sweet little pussy. True to Kiki's word, she gave Fantasia a place to sit upon her face, her mouth sucking and licking her friend to multiple orgasms. Duncan and Fantasia faced each other atop Kiki's body, their hands touching each other's hands as they fondled and squeezed Kiki's enormous breasts. Duncan was mesmerized watching Fantasia's face as she orgasmed, it giving him almost as much pleasure as fucking Kiki.

He slid his hands up Fantasia's body and took hold of her breasts. She smiled and leaned into him. He leaned forward so his face was only inches from hers and she didn't move

18

away. Another orgasm rippled through her body and he felt her breath when she moaned in delight. He leaned closer and put his lips upon hers. She accepted him and kissed back. He slipped his tongue into her mouth and she began to suck on it and he moaned in ecstasy as he orgasmed and Kiki's hips bucked against his and she too was crying out in bliss beneath Fantasia's pussy.

A little while later all three of them were lying in bed, Kiki uncuffed, all of their limbs tangled, all of them with satisfied grins. "I like you, you're a lot of fun," Kiki said to Duncan and patted his semi hard cock. "Don't worry, I have more blue pills. I'm going to step outside for a cigarette and when I come back it's your turn." She leaned over and kissed him, bit his lower lip, then hopped out of bed. "Come keep me company, girlfriend."

Fantasia leaned over and kissed Duncan and he was in heaven as he watched the two beautiful goddesses slip on their outfits and step outside the motel door.

VIII

He didn't know how life could get any better. Having been an accountant for almost twenty years he began to calculate at three thousand dollars a night, how long he could live this night over and over with Fantasia and Kiki. A little over eight months...but that wasn't counting the price of hotels and food. The thought was tempting but he needed that money to get away and truly start a whole new life. He wondered what it would take to change Fantasia's mind. She'd already changed it once when she kissed him after she said she didn't do that. Maybe that was the start, the crack in the dike, as they say. He laughed at the thought of dyke's cracks.

"What's so funny?" Kiki asked with a smile as the ladies came back into the room. She and Fantasia immediately slipped out of their clothes.

19

"I was just thinking about what a wonderful life this is," Duncan replied.

"Well we have a special treat for you," Kiki said as she moved to the bed.

"See what I mean, it just keeps getting better and better," he said.

"Give me your hand," Kiki told him. He raised up his right arm and Kiki clasped it in one of the pink handcuffs attached to the headboard. She climbed onto the bed and reached over him, her large breasts brushing against his chest and face. "Now the other one," she said, reaching for his left arm.

Duncan looked at Fantasia who was still standing near the door, her arms hugging herself, her smile having fallen away. "Hold on a sec," Duncan said.

Kiki grabbed his free hand and said, "Come on, be a good boy."

"No, wait. Stop," he said and tried to pull his free hand away. Kiki grabbed him harder. Duncan began to struggle.

"Grab his legs!" Kiki yelled to Fantasia. Duncan glanced at her and she looked like a deer in the headlights. Kiki yelled again and Fantasia finally bolted forward and grabbed Duncan's ankles trying to immobilize him.

"No!" Duncan yelled and twisted his body and swung his left fist at Kiki's head. She was knocked backwards off the bed and into the wall next to the nightstand. Fantasia clung to his ankles and he saw a look of fear and sadness painted across her face. He jerked his left leg free and then kicked out and hit Fantasia in the hip, knocking her to the floor.

Fantasia's eyes grew large and she screamed, "Don't hurt him!"

Out of the corner of his eye he caught movement coming from Kiki but it was too late as he saw the flash of the black billy club and then there was nothingness.

Duncan awoke to a much too bright room and a throbbing in his head like someone was banging a gong in it over and over again. He went to touch the sore spot on the side of his head but realized his right hand was still attached to the wagon wheel by the pink handcuffs. With his free left hand he gently touched the side of his head and winced. His hair was blood encrusted over his right ear and a sizeable goose egg had risen up.

He heard more knocking but ascertained it was coming from outside his head, not within. Bright sunlight pushed into the room from around the ratty curtains and it looked like a tornado had whipped through the room. The blankets, sheets and bedspread were strewn across the floor along with clumps of towels, his clothes and shoes, plastic cups with splotches of drink that had spilled out. Atop the dresser sat the opened, half eaten box of pizza and the two liter bottle of Coke laying on its side without its cap and most of its contents puddled on the floor. The bottle of Captain Morgan was not left behind.

Another knock came from the motel door and then the door swung open. Painfully bright sunlight shot into the room and washed over the floor, the bed, the back wall. Duncan brought up his left arm to shield his eyes from the onslaught as if he were a vampire afraid of the sun.

"Housekeeping!" a plump little Mexican lady said and then froze two steps into the room as if she had hit an invisible wall. Her eyes grew wide when she saw the naked gringo handcuffed to the bed, dried blood on his face, arm and bed. "Dios mio!" she said putting her hands to her mouth and taking a step back.

"No, wait!" Duncan said as he tugged against his restraints. "Help me. I need a key," he said pointing to the handcuffs with his free hand.

"No, senor," the housekeeper said and did the sign of the cross over her chest. "I call police."

"No!" Duncan exclaimed as she turned around and then all sunlight into the room was blocked by two large figures in the doorway. "Oh shit," Duncan mumbled and backed up against the headboard.

Croak was first to walk into the motel room and he pushed the housekeeper into the lone chair between the bed and window. "Be still," he told her and then he looked to the bed, shaking his head slowly. "Duncan, what are you doing?" He was wearing his poncho and faded skinny jeans and the daylight highlighted the various colors of browns, golds, reds and yellows interspersed throughout his dark dreadlocks.

"It looks like Duncan was having the time of his life," BC said as he stepped into the room, almost having to turn sideways to get his large bulk through the door. He wore a dark blue Fubu outfit with gold pinstriping.

"Where's my money?" Croak asked.

"It's in the trunk of my car."

"And where's your car?"

Oh shit, Duncan thought.

X

Duncan was sitting in the back of a red Nissan Pathfinder from Hertz and they were travelling a desert highway into Las Vegas. A million and one scenarios played through Duncan's mind, all of them bad. Croak sat in the driver's seat and BC next to him in the passenger's seat and neither of them paying Duncan any mind that he could be a threat behind them. He had looked around the vehicle to see if there was anything he might use as a weapon that he could knock them out with blows to the head like he had been knocked out. But he'd given up on the idea when he considered nothing short of a three foot long pipe swung with full range of motion would even phase BC, and even that might just make him mad.

22

"What were you thinking?" Croak asked from the front seat. "You had to know we'd come looking for you."

"I don't know," Duncan replied shaking his head. Even that action made his bruised skull throb. "There was just so much of it, I didn't think you would miss it."

"I'm not going to care almost a million dollars is missing?"

"I just thought you'd print up more, no big deal."

"No big deal? Do you have any idea how much work and time is required in such an endeavor? That's ten thousand squares, ten thousand serial numbers, three color process, double sided, security strips, watermarks, ultraviolet inks. And those bills are not casino quality. You really fucked me."

"I'm sorry," Duncan said. "I didn't mean to--"

"And I don't like to be fucked. You better be right about those girls," Croak said coldly.

"Duncan, can I ask you something?" BC asked. "Is that Asian pussy sideways?" His laughter bellowed within the truck.

Duncan looked out the side window at the brown desert rushing by at seventy miles an hour. He wondered if he could survive a leap from the truck, but even if he did - which he probably wouldn't - where could he run to in the middle of nowhere? His only hope was to get into the city and find an opportunity to get away. Either that or really get lucky and locate Fantasia and Kiki as he told Croak he could.

XI

"This is the place?" Croak asked.

They were standing amidst the galleria of high end shops attached to the Aria Resort and Casino in the middle of the Las Vegas strip. In front of them was the Jimmy Choo shoe store with window displays of lady's footwear costing at least four figures. Inside the shop a lone attendant was working and looked like he could be a descendant of the flamboyant Elton John, down to his bedazzled, gem encrusted glasses.

23

"How can I help you boys?" the salesperson asked as he stood with his hand on his hip. His name tag read: Roy.

"We're looking for a couple ladies," Duncan said.

"That's a shame," Roy said with a sway of his shoulders. His eyes kept drifting to BC, from the waist down.

"A tall blonde and a short Asian with big tits."

"You just described half of Vegas."

"Stop fucking around," Croak said. "Were they here or not?"

Roy's jaw dropped. "Excuse me, Mr. Eastwood, but that language is not appreciated here."

Croak stepped toward the man and looked down at him and said coldly, "Then you're really not going to appreciate what happens next if you don't tell me what I want to know."

Roy swallowed a lump of fear and looked around the store for a lifeline but there was only the three men in front of him barring any chance of escape. He looked into Croak's gray eyes and said, "I think they might have been here. About an hour ago."

"Any idea where they went?"

"They could have gone anywhere."

"Guess."

Roy's lip trembled and he looked like he was about to cry. "W-well the Asian girl said something about Victoria's Secret. That's all I know, r-really."

"How much money did they spend here?"

"Wh-wh-what?" When Croak didn't repeat himself, he finally said, "About eight thousand."

Croak nodded to BC. BC grabbed Roy's bony elbow and said very politely, "I'm going to need you to retrieve that money for me."

As he led the salesperson to the cash register, Roy asked, "What about my commission?"

"How long do you think it will be until they find him in the storeroom?" Duncan asked.

"Not my problem," Croak replied. "Make the call."

They had walked fifty yards through the array of shops away from the Jimmy Choo store and stopped in front of Golden Vein Coffee and Toffee shop. BC held his notepad computer, piggybacking off the shop's wifi signal, and nodded to Duncan.

Duncan had called Fantasia's number a half dozen times since they had gotten on the strip and were in range of a wifi signal. He now knew how they had located him so quickly and he kicked himself for being so stupid. He pressed 'Call' on his phone and listened to it ring but knowing she wouldn't answer. She had played him for a chump and gotten what she wanted, so there was no reason for her to--

"Duncan? I'm sorry, I didn't know--" was all he heard of her sweet voice before the phone was snatched from his grasp.

"Where's my fucking money, bitch?" Croak growled into the phone.

Duncan tried to grab his phone back but Croak shoved him away and then BC held him in a one armed bear hug that immobilized him.

"Fuck!" Croak said and threw the phone at Duncan. It bounced off his chest and landed on the floor. Croak looked at BC. "Did we get her?"

"Ping!" BC said with a smile, the lights glinting off his gold tooth. "They're at the Miracle Mile shops just across the strip."

They made their way to street level and across the busy eight lane strip and minutes later walked into one of the two entrances into the complex known as Miracle Mile. In the middle of the conglomeration of fifty or sixty shops was the Planet Hollywood Casino. All of the shops looped around the sides and back of the casino in a horseshoe formation and thousands of Las Vegas tourists flocked in and out of all the businesses.

"I don't want any bullshit," Croak mumbled to Duncan. "As soon as you see them, you point them out to us."

Duncan nodded his head but kept hearing Fantasia's last words in his head: I'm sorry. What was she sorry about? Did she mean it or was she just saying that? Would Croak hurt her or just take his money and leave? For that matter, whether Croak did or didn't get all his money, Duncan had to wonder what was going to happen to him. Croak wasn't the type of guy to let something like that go unpunished and the only reason he hadn't done anything to him was because he needed Duncan to find the girls.

"I need to use the restroom," Duncan said as they stepped out of the desert heat and into the air conditioned complex.

"It can wait," Croak told him.

"No, it can't."

Croak glared at him and realized Duncan wasn't wavering. "Fine!" he said and looked around until he saw an arrow pointing towards restrooms in the casino. The three of them walked through the Planet Hollywood Casino floor, the bells and jingles of slot machines, voices of joy and defeat, exclamations of surprise, dealers calling out "Blackjack!", cheers and clapping, music being piped in through the speakers, the building filled with nonstop action. BC accompanied Duncan into the restroom while Croak stood outside eyeing every blonde and Asian he saw.

XIII

"What's going to happen to me?" Duncan asked as he relieved himself at the urinal.

BC looked at him and said, "I don't know, little man. Maybe you should have thought about that before you stole the money."

"What about the girls?"

"Croak just wants his money back."

When they walked out of the bathroom they found Croak standing still as a statue, his eyes locked onto something across the casino floor about thirty yards away. "There, is that them?" he asked, his voice barely a whisper.

"No, I don't think so," Duncan said, not quite sure what he was looking at. And then he saw them. "Holy shit," he mumbled, not believing his eyes. He really didn't believe he'd ever see them again, but there they were jumping up and down at a craps table, laughing and hugging each other, their backs to them.

"That's them, isn't it?" Croak said.

Duncan wanted to lie but the look on his face was unmistakable.

"Come on," Croak said and began walking forward. Duncan seemed frozen in his spot until BC gave him a nudge. As they drew closer Duncan saw that they were both wearing skin tight black dresses and he watched their asses bounce as they jumped up and down in glee. At their feet were a dozen shopping bags from as many different stores. They had wasted no time in going on their shopping spree. After a roll of the dice he heard Kiki's squeal of delight and he saw her and Fantasia's side profiles as they jumped and hugged and squished their tits together. Duncan felt a tingle in his groin as he eye fucked Fantasia, remembering the most amazing night of his life.

The two women were oblivious to anyone around them as the three men approached. Croak nodded at BC and the big black man clasped his hand onto Kiki's arm. Croak grabbed Fantasia.

"Let go of my arm, fat boy!" Kiki said as she turned around.

"Hey!" Fantasia said as she unsuccessfully tried to pull her arm away from Croak. She sucked in her breath when she saw Duncan. Kiki saw him at the same time.

"What are you doing here? How did you find us?" Kiki asked.

27

"Come on," Croak said, tugging on Fantasia's arm.

"I'm not going with you," Fantasia said to the tall, skinny dreadlocked man. Her eyes went to Duncan as if pleading for help.

Kiki tried to grab onto the craps table but BC merely picked her up off the ground as if she were no bigger than a Chihuahua. "Let me go!" she screamed.

Everyone around the craps table backed up and others in the casino were turning their attention to the commotion. A security guard, stocky with a crew cut looking as if he just came from the military, approached BC and said, "Sir, put the lady down."

BC slipped the Asian under his left arm and held her as if she were a bag of potatoes. Her tiny dress slipped up her waist exposing her bare ass and pussy to all behind them. With his right arm BC picked up the guard and threw him onto the craps table causing chips and dice to fly into the air.

Two more security guards and a pit boss appeared and tried to take BC down and having next to no luck in their endeavor. One of them was trying to pull Kiki from his grasp but only managed to free her breasts from her dress.

Without another thought, Duncan swung his elbow across the bridge of Croak's nose and then he grabbed Fantasia's wrist and yanked her away. Croak screamed in pain and anger as blood spurted from his face. His hand slipped beneath his poncho and reappeared holding the large chrome revolver.

People started screaming. "Gun! Gun!" From somewhere in the casino a voice of authority was hollering, "Drop the gun! Drop the gun now!"

Duncan ran through the casino holding onto Fantasia's hand and she ran with him offering no resistance. There was the sound of gunfire behind them and then the entire casino was filled with screams and everybody running for the two exits. A stampede of people pressed against Duncan and Fantasia and her hand slipped from his as they ran. Before he could turn back and see where she was he felt her small hand

28

grasp his. Duncan smiled as he pushed through the doors to outside with Fantasia at his side.

XIV

"Over there!" Duncan said and led Fantasia down a set of steps to street level. They ran to a taxi waiting at a red light. The doors were locked and both of them pounded on the windows.

A voice bellowed from behind them. "Duncan! I'm coming for you!" He looked back to see Croak standing in the doorway of Miracle Mile, his face covered in blood and more blood pouring from a gunshot in his shoulder. He was parting a sea of people like Moses as he brought up his chrome revolver from beneath his poncho.

Duncan heard the electronic locks of the taxi doors disengage and he yanked open the door and pushed Fantasia inside, not missing the fact that she was pantiless beneath her black dress. He dove in on top of her as the roar of the gun exploded and the rear window of the taxi shattered and crumbled into a thousand sparkling pieces.

The Middle Eastern taxi driver looked over his shoulder in shock.

"Drive! Drive!" Duncan screamed.

The driver punched the gas and shot through the red light, sending other cars swerving and slamming on their brakes.

Duncan looked out the shattered back window to see Croak being tackled from the side by security and police officers.

"Fantasia, are you okay?" Duncan asked.

She sat up brushing glass chips from her hair. She nodded and looked at Duncan. "It's Renae." When he looked at her like a confused puppy she said, "My name's Renae."

"We need to get out of town," Duncan told her.

The taxi pulled to a side street and the driver yelled at them to get out of his car. Duncan handed him a few hundred dollar bills and said, "Just take us to my car." He asked Renae where it was and she told him. The driver complied unhappily.

"Why do I need to get out of town?" Renae asked.

"Because you've been passing counterfeit money all over town."

"What!? The money's not real? You were going to pay me last night with fake money?" she asked and hit him on the arm.

The driver held one of the hundred dollar bills up to his window. "Don't worry, those ones are real," Duncan lied to him. To Renae he said, "What do you mean? You and Kiki tried to rob me!"

"It wasn't my idea," she said. "Kiki was just going to handcuff you and leave you there. I didn't know you'd get hurt. Are you okay?"

"I don't know. Will you come to Miami with me?"

She looked at him and the desire in his eyes. "Well, I do have an aunt in Georgia I haven't visited in a while."

"That makes me feel a little better," he told her.

"I can make you feel a lot better," Renae told him with a smile.

"You already are. You already are."

Duncan's phone rang and he quickly threw it out the back window of the taxi. He took Renae's phone and did the same.

Part 2

Dirty Dancers

I

She had honey-colored skin that he was sure tasted just as sweet as it hovered and undulated only inches from his face. His eyes were on the little black hole of her belly button as it swirled 'round and 'round and then drifted down to the ocean blue g-string that wasn't much bigger than an eye patch.

"My eyes are up here," Trixie joked in her squeaky college girl voice that still had two weeks to go before starting her first semester at UNLV.

"I'm not paying twenty dollars to look into your eyes," her customer mumbled playfully.

"What you're looking at costs a lot more than twenty," Trixie said.

"I know." The song ended and another began. "Keep dancing."

She did as requested, pushing her bare breasts into his face and getting his attention. Trixie had large, firm natural breasts which was something that set her apart among many strippers in Vegas with all their plastic parts. Unfortunately, she had a glass eye in place of her left orb and a scar running from the eye socket to the hairline at her temple, the result of a playground accident when she was six. The deformity kept her from getting jobs at high end gentlemen's clubs which was why she was working at Paddy's Playhouse in the shadows of old Vegas.

Gary Taggart preferred the hole in the wall strip clubs more than the upscale spots because he found the women to be more genuinely friendly as well as more apt to give a little more play during the lap dances and in the back rooms. Every now and then he could get lucky and even meet with one of the girls outside the club for some real action.

Taggart was a fit six feet tall with a bald head that he was self-conscious about but most women seemed to find sexy on him. He was dressed casually in jeans and a black button-up short sleeved shirt and some black leather loafers. In the rear of his waistband, tucked in a hideaway pancake holster, was a small 9mm Sig Sauer semiautomatic handgun.

Trixie put her hands on the customer's shiny white dome and painted his face with her titties, her perky nipples brushing across his nose, eyes and chin. She pressed her leg against his crotch and his hardness told her she was doing something right. She felt his hands slide up the side of her legs and over her hips. Touching wasn't technically allowed in any Vegas strip club, but it went on all the time, especially if you wanted to get good tips. And there were even more ways to really get good tips, something Trixie had been perfecting to a fine art because she had her heart set on a new white Mercedes Benz.

She put her head next to Taggart's and swirled her tongue around the inside of her customer's ear and felt him press into her, his hands squeezing her hips. "Are you enjoying yourself?" she asked in a sultry whisper, her breath hot against his skin. When he mumbled in the affirmative she stroked her leg up and down his excited crotch and asked, "Do you really want to enjoy yourself?"

"I really do," he told her. "How much?"

"A hundred."

"Okay."

"Okay," she said and slid herself down his body like he was a waterslide. Her dark brown curly hair fell down in his lap and he was really curious to see what his hundred dollars was going to buy him. In the past two years that he had begun frequenting the myriad of Las Vegas strip clubs he'd experienced almost every form of pleasure from a twenty dollar lap dance to a five hundred dollar blowjob in the backroom to a hundred and seventy five dollar fuck in the ladies' restroom. Everything in Vegas was for sale for a price and that price was always negotiable.

Taggart felt pressure on his cock through the fabric of his jeans and then felt the heat of her breath engulfing him. She had put her mouth over him and was breathing heavily through the denim; it was making him hard as can be straining against his jeans. She looked up at him and smiled into his alcohol muddled blue eyes that were a little darker than her g-string. He felt himself sinking into her mud brown eyes.

Trixie stood up, running her hands up his chest and touching his face before turning around and bending over to give him a perfect view of her sweet ass cheeks with the ribbon of blue fabric running up her crack and splitting into a Y to loop over her hips. She looked over her shoulder looking at him ogling her ass and she smiled when his eyes grew wide as she grabbed her ass cheeks and spread them apart. She lowered herself into his lap and wiggled her ass cheeks from side to side until his hard cock beneath his jeans was centered perfectly in her ass crack and then she let her cheeks go.

"Ooh!" Taggart moaned pleasantly as her ass seemed to clamp onto his shaft. He was lost in sensation and oblivious to how many songs played over the club's sound system. A couple of times the DJ spoke but all Taggart heard was the sound of Charlie Brown's teacher. Trixie began to slide her ass up and down and Taggart clenched his ass cheeks in rhythm to her movement. He was in heaven as he brought his hands to her hips and pulled her into him with each thrust.

"Oh yeah, that's nice, isn't it?" she cooed.

"Oh yeah," he replied breathlessly.

His hips began to move faster and so did her ass bouncing up and down in his lap but keeping him firmly grasped in her crack. She grabbed his hands from her hips and pulled them up and around to firmly grasp her large bouncing tits.

"Oh yes," she breathed. "Come on, baby. Oh yes."

Taggart gritted his teeth and squeezed her titties hard as his pelvis rattled against her ass and he nutted in his tightie-whities. His hands slipped down her sides and rested on her thighs and she leaned her head back onto his shoulder and asked, "Did you like?"

"Yes I did," he replied before she kissed him on the cheek and then stood up looking for her blue bikini top. Taggart remained seated a moment to let everything settle and then he slowly stood up from the loveseat and pulled out his wallet. He handed her a hundred dollars and she smiled.

"Don't forget about the songs," she said batting her big brown eyes.

"Oh yeah, how many?"

"Four."

He pulled out four twenties and handed them to her.

"And my tip."

He gave her two more twenties.

"Thank you baby," she said and gave him a hug. "Let me know if you want to have more fun," and then she disappeared into the club and through an Employees Only door.

Taggart patted his jeans to make sure nothing had splotched through. He used to wear designer boxer briefs but found they often soaked through; tightie-whities alleviated that problem and let him continue enjoying the night.

II

Taggart grabbed his drink from the small cocktail table and downed the last of what was mostly melted ice. He set the glass down and made his way from the dark back corner of the club where he'd gotten his dance. One other man was in the shadows a few seats down being pleased by a tall, skinny black woman with pancake breasts. Taggart focused on the bar at the other end of the club and made a beeline for it.

Paddy's Playhouse was small for Vegas standards with room for maybe sixty patrons and not quite half full this

Wednesday night. Unlike other clubs that might have multiple rooms or multiple floors, PP's, as the locals called it, consisted of one large boxy space with a stage and a stripper pole jutting out from one wall out to the center of the club. The bar was located along the wall near the entrance with small tables and chairs scattered around the three sides of the stage. A row of chairs was pushed up all along the edge of the stage, known affectionately as Sniffer's Row, and in the far back corners of the club were half a dozen loveseats for the private lap dances.

"Get your dollars out for Kassidy stepping up on stage," bellowed the DJ from his booth between the bar and stage. A dozen other girls, scantily clad, worked the floor smoozing customers and two drink girls in black leotards rushed back and forth from the tables and bars.

Taggart was halfway across the club when Kassidy jumped up onto the pole and spun around, her light brown hair in a long pony tail. Taggart stopped to check her out, admiring the most perfectly toned ass he'd ever seen. She had the legs and arms of a gymnast and she worked the pole like it was her bitch and Taggart thought she was too good to be in a place like PP's. But then she flung her top off and he realized why she was here: she was practically flat chested, the only bumps being her two rosy pink nipples.

Maybe she's working here to save up to get a boob job, Taggart thought. He turned back toward the bar but then something caught his attention and he looked at the stage where three college aged guys were laughing and having the time of their lives, tossing dollar bills onto the stage like they were confetti. Other men were tossing bills onto stage as well but what caught Taggart's eye was that these three men's bills glowed as white as ghosts beneath the stage's black lights.

Taggart squeezed his way through tables and chairs until he was standing behind the three frat boys. They were oblivious to his presence and continued to toss counterfeit one dollar bills onto the stage where Kassidy dismounted from the pole into the splits.

"Excuse me, gentlemen," Taggart said.

One of the three stooges glanced over his shoulder and said, "Go away, old man," and turned his attention back to the stripper on stage.

Old man? Taggart thought. I'm only thirty-seven. He reached into his pocket and pulled out a gold badge emblazoned with U.S. Treasury Department. "How fucking stupid do you have to be to counterfeit one dollar bills?" Taggart said.

Two of the college kids' heads jerked around to see the badge. The one who had commented on Taggart's age was lost in Kassidy's booty that was bobbing up and down in front of his face.

"Oh shit!" one of the men said and then both bolted from their chairs toward the door. The third in their trio realized their absence and then saw Taggart's badge. The kid swung a wild haymaker which the Treasury agent easily ducked. Using the momentum of the kid's swing, he spun him around and bashed his forehead into the edge of the stage - twice, so he knew what this old man could do. Kassidy didn't get upset until the agent began scooping the illegal tender off the stage to be confiscated for evidence.

III

It was nearly one thirty in the morning when Taggart pulled his blue Ford Taurus into the empty two car garage. The garage door closed behind him as he stepped through the door into the kitchen, his footsteps echoing in the empty house. He and his soon to be ex-wife had purchased the three bedroom, two bathroom home three years ago. It was situated in a family friendly neighborhood in North Las Vegas that seemed ideal for their two boys, seven and eight, and their little girl who was five. Taggart walked past his dark Dell laptop sitting on the kitchen counter, past the bare dining room and turned the corner and walked upstairs to the master bedroom as he did so many nights since Angie had left with the kids nine months ago.

The master suite was empty, as were the other two bedrooms in the house, save for a pile of dirty clothes in front of the walk-in closet. A couple of weeks after Angie had taken the kids back to their hometown in Ohio a large moving van arrived with four stout workers who had proceeded to pack up everything except Taggart's clothes and his favorite recliner. In the master bathroom Taggart emptied his pockets onto the counter, along with his holstered gun, and then threw his clothes in the dirty pile and took a shower.

Twenty minutes later he was in a clean pair of tightie-whities and lounging in his recliner in the middle of the vacant living room. Next to his chair was an upended empty box for a table which had a half full bottle of Grey Goose vodka and the television remote. He grabbed the remote and brought to life the 42" flat screen that sat atop two stacked empty boxes six feet in front of his chair. Some show that he thought he might have seen before was on HBO and he let it play. He traded the remote for the bottle, pulled a gray blanket over him and settled into his chair until sleep came.

IV

"Thirty eighty dollars," Lyman Cope, chief of the Las Vegas bureau of the U.S. Treasury Department, said. "You gave some kid a concussion for thirty eight dollars."

Taggart was sitting in a leather upholstered chair in the chief's office. "He assaulted me, purely self-defense. And the bills were bogus. It was a good collar. I figured I'd interview him today and then go pick up his friends."

Cope shook his head. "I've already got Magnusson and Perez on it."

"But it was my collar," Taggart said defensively.

The chief was nearing sixty with a head of salt and pepper hair and he sat on the edge of his desk as he often did when speaking to his agents. He came off as more of a concerned father than a boss. "What were you doing in that place?"

Cope had a way of making Taggart feel like an uncomfortable teenager. "I was off duty. Is that why you're taking me off the case, because I was at some titty bar?"

"Don't use that language." Cope was a god fearing, church going family man who'd never seen the inside of a strip club. "I'm concerned about you. Your actions and behavior reflect me and the department. Have you seen the person I referred to you?"

Six months ago, after learning of Taggart's wife leaving, Cope had given him the name of a counselor. Taggart had gone to two appointments to see the bookish, bland woman and even though she wasn't much to look at he still wondered what she would look like swinging on a stripper pole. He didn't tell her this, of course, and he minimized his patronage of strip clubs and said nothing of the extras he sought out, and still she commented that he might be dealing with a form of sex addiction. He didn't really agree with her and even if he did, he didn't think it was such a bad thing. He hadn't been back to see her in four months.

"Yes, I've seen her," Taggart said. "I don't do anything that makes our agency look bad. I do my job and I do it well and I deserve to investigate my bust."

"Your bust is chicken scratchings, kids with laser printers. That's why I gave it to Magnusson." Taggart was about to protest but the chief kept talking. "You're my best agent and despite your family problems it hasn't seemed to hamper your job performance. I have something big for you." The chief reached into his desk drawer and pulled out a large clear plastic evidence bag stuffed with hundred dollar bills which he placed in front of Taggart.

Taggart opened the bag and removed one of the counterfeit hundreds, impressed with the craftsmanship and feel of the bill. Chief Cope opened a file folder and said, "Two days ago two women were spending these hundreds in shops at Miracle Mile. They managed to spend almost eighteen thousand in two hours. One of the women was arrested at the Planet Hollywood Casino, Amanda Chin, goes by the name of Kiki."

"A stripper?"

"An escort. The other woman, Renae Savoy is an escort named Fantasia. She got away."

"How'd they grab one and not the other?" Taggart asked.

Cope handed him 8X10 photos of the two women - one a short, busty Asian and the other a tall, thin blonde, both very beautiful. "That's where it gets interesting. The women were accosted at the craps table by three men, one of whom pulled a gun."

"I heard about the shooting at the casino. Wasn't one of the perps killed?"

"No. He was shot in the shoulder and then taken down on the strip as he tried to shoot at one of the fleeing men or Miss Savoy or both." Cope handed Taggart more 8X10 photos from casino surveillance of the three men - one a clean cut white male, one who looked like a black refrigerator in a Fubu outfit, and the third like he was from a spaghetti western wearing a poncho and wielding a large chrome revolver.

"So these three men were together or not together?"

"We're not sure. Nobody's talking. The African American is Percy Johns and he had eight thousand dollars of counterfeit bills in his possession. He and Miss Chin bailed out of county a little after midnight, as soon as their thirty six hours were up."

"And the other two men?"

"The cowboy is Allyn Simpson, forty-one, from Oregon known affectionately as Croak."

"Croak?"

"Croak. He's currently in ICU at county medical under police watch. And we don't know who the last male figure is. But we do know he and Miss Savoy left in a taxi together and the taxi driver was irate to find out he'd been paid in bogus bills. He threatened to sue the government if we didn't reimburse him. He said he dropped the couple off at a parking garage a block from the strip. We're reviewing security cameras but nothing yet."

Taggart reviewed the photo files he'd been handed, spending a little extra time examining the two missing players: Average Joe and the hot blonde. "Do we have an address on Savoy?"

"Yes, the Airedale Trailer Park."

"And what's the status on Croak?"

Chief Cope shook his head at the ridiculous street name. "He'll be in ICU at least until this evening and possibly until tomorrow."

"I'm on it," Taggart said as he got up from the chair.

V

"Get on it then!" Taggart said as he sat on the futon couch with his pants and underwear pulled down and bunched at his ankles. The petite redhead with a constellation of freckles across her nose and cheeks giggled as she pulled off her peach colored thong and threw it across the trailer at him. He let the small article of fabric hit him in the side of the head and it caught and hung from his ear. Stacy laughed hysterically at the sight as she leaped toward him. He watched her happy b-cup breasts bounce toward him and then his eyes settled on the fiery patch of hair at her crotch.

"Do you like my fire crotch?" she asked as she stood on the creaky futon, her legs on either side of him. She wiggled it in his face.

Taggart reached up and clasped her tight ass cheeks in his hands and pulled her muff to his face. He half expected it to taste like a cinnamon Red Hot candy; it didn't, though she was hot. He liked the feel of her soft, fuzzy bush tickling his nose and upper lip and he realized this was the first time he'd ever felt such sensations. Every woman he'd been with was either

40

clean shaven or had well manicured and groomed little landing strips or such.

"I guess you do," Stacy said as she plucked her thong from his ear and dropped it to the floor behind her. "Ohhh, that's nice," meaning both his mouth on her pussy and his hands squeezing her ass and spreading her ass cheeks.

Taggart's hungry tongue moved up and down her protruding labia lips and then delved into her moist, pink hole. He moved his head from side to side as his tongue wiggled back and forth inside her. His strong hands massaged her ass cheeks in gyrating circles, grinding her pelvis into his face even harder.

Stacy's pussy became hotter and wetter as he found his groove and the top of his tongue moved up and down like a heart monitor pulse, brushing against her excited clit on every up stroke.

"I like how you do that," she moaned as she braced her hands on his muscular shoulders. Her thighs began to quiver in delight. "Oh sweet Jesus, yes!" she panted. His mouth and tongue didn't waver from its mesmerizing pace and the excitement built up within her like a coiled spring. Unlike many men who thought that they should quicken their pace or go harder when a woman neared climax, Taggart knew to stay in the same groove, the same pressure, the same motion once you found her secret combination. If there was one thing he could thank his ex-wife for it was helping him become a world class pussy eater.

Stacy screamed and pushed Taggart's head back against the futon with her pelvis. The spring that had coiled up inside her had let loose and felt like it was bouncing around wildly inside her as her ass spasmed uncontrollably in his grasp and her pussy thumped against his face. She screamed again and again and Taggart was glad that the heavy rock group Disturbed was pounding through her stereo system and masking her cries or else someone would surely be calling the police. He would find this one a little hard to explain to his chief.

Thirty minutes earlier Taggart had pulled into Airedale Trailer Park located on the east side of Las Vegas. The park was cleaner than he expected - no dilapidated trailers or cars up on blocks - and it reminded him of a retirement community. He found the address of the double wide trailer that he had for Renae Savoy and he parked his Taurus crossways behind the two cars under the carport to keep either of them from making a hasty exit.

He sat in his car for a moment exploring the trailer and surrounding trailers and roadway. The beige trailer looked relatively new with no dents or dings in its siding, no cracked windows, and no trash littering the outside. There were two access points he could see, both on the same side of the trailer. The door toward the back end of the trailer was closed and had three simple wooden steps that led down to the gray gravel behind the carport. An eight foot redwood deck with a couple of lawn chairs painted the color of the rainbow was in front of the front door with steps leading to the edge of the carport.

Taggart turned off the car and heard the distant rumble of hard rock music. He stepped out of the car and determined the sound was coming through the screen door of the trailer. He adjusted the gun at the rear of his waistband of his blue slacks as he looked at the two cars under the carport. On the left was a pristine eighties Corvette as yellow as the sun with a vanity plate that read HOTSPNR. Beside it was a silver Hyundai Elantra only a year or two old with regular Nevada tags.

The music volume grew louder as he climbed the steps to the deck and he could feel the thump of the bass in his chest as he neared the screen door. Taggart kept glancing toward the door at the rear of the trailer as well as looking for movement in the trailer windows. He reached the screen door and stood off to the side before peering inside and seeing the last thing in the world he expected to see.

In the middle of the living room was a stripper pole from floor to ceiling and upon said stripper pole was a petite lady in her early thirties with wavy red hair past her shoulders. She wore a peach colored thong and nothing else as she performed amazing feats on the pole, some of which Taggart had never seen in all his club hopping. He stood in awe of her talent and had forgotten what he'd come there for. The music ended as she finished a flurry of pole spins that culminated in a backwards handstand dismount from the pole and then she whipped her hair back and threw her hands in the air. Taggart couldn't help but clap his hands.

"Hey!" she said as she spun around in surprise to face the screen door. She made no move to cover her exposed breasts. "Who are you?" she asked fearlessly approaching and opening the screen door.

Taggart spun on his heel to avoid getting hit by the flimsy aluminum and mesh door. As he did so he pulled his badge from his pocket and showed it to her as he said, "I'm Special Agent Taggart, ma'am, with the U.S. Treasury Department. I'm looking for Renae Savoy. Does she live here?"

"She's not here," the redhead said as she looked up at him. She was about 5'4" with green hazel eyes and thin lips. "How long have you been standing there watching me?"

"Not long enough," Taggart replied and she smiled. "Do one of those cars belong to Miss Savoy?"

"Her's is the Elantra," the topless lady told him. "The Vette is mine."

"Of course it is. And what's your name?"

"Stacy. Stacy O'Malley," she said and stuck out her right hand.

He shook it, surprised at the strength of her tiny hand. "Gary," he said though not exactly sure why. He kept finding it difficult to not let his eyes settle on her almost neon pink nipples that were obviously in an excited state.

"Special agent," she said, emphasizing the special.

"Yes. You say Renae is not here? Would you mind if I--"

"Come in and look," Stacy said at the same time he spoke. She remained standing in the doorway holding open the screen door and as he stepped inside his bare arm brushed

43

against one of her nipples. His body felt like it touched a live wire.

Despite the beautiful attraction beside him that smelled of cinnamon and rose, Taggart's eyes immediately went to the back of the trailer where the door would be. There was a long hallway running the length of the trailer on the left hand side and he could see daylight coming through the backdoor window, but no one had tried to make an escape when he entered.

"When was the last time you saw Miss Savoy?" Taggart asked.

"A few days ago."

"Is that common?"

"Yeah. We work different schedules and sometimes she travels for her job and I might not see her for a week."

"And what's her job?"

"If you're a special agent I'd think you'd know the answer already."

Taggart nodded and smiled before asking, "What do you do?"

"For work?"

No, for fun, Taggart thought but said nothing.

"I do personal training and some personal assistant work."

Taggart wondered if that was code for prostitution. "Is that all?" he asked.

"What?" Stacy looked at him, her smile dissipating. "I'm not a hooker, if that's what you're insinuating."

"Not at all," Taggart lied. He nodded toward the stripper pole. "I thought maybe you were an exotic dancer. You were really good."

Her smile returned, bigger and brighter than before. "Thank you. I used to work the clubs a few years ago but now I just compete in international pole dancing competitions. I've won two titles so far."

"I believe it."

"That's so nice," she said and put her hand on his bicep. "Would you like to see the routine I'm working on?"

"I would. But first would it be okay if I search the trailer?"

"You don't believe me?"

"I'm just doing my job."

"Do you have a gun?" Stacy asked and looked at his waist and a little below.

"Yes. Yes I do," he said and eyed her body up and down and feeling a tingling in his groin. "Am I going to need it to search the trailer?"

"There's no one here but us."

"Let me make sure of that."

She looked up at him and gave a cute little pout before telling him Renae's room was at the back of the trailer. Taggart checked every room and closet and then returned to the living room where Stacy had made them both some vodka and cranberries.

"I'm on duty," he told her.

"I won't tell if you won't."

VII

As they finished their drinks Taggart asked if Stacy had any idea where Renae might be, who her friends and relatives were, Renae's phone number, and finally he showed her a photo on his phone of the Average Joe and asked if she knew him or had seen him, which Stacy had not.

"Okay, you promised," she said, taking his glass away from him and sitting him on the futon couch in the living room.

As she got the music prepped for her routine Taggart said, "I don't know that I've seen someone work the pole to Disturbed."

"I know," she smiled giddily. "The extreme always makes an impression. Ready?"

45

Taggart nodded his head, the music started, and Stacy went wild on the pole, arms, legs and hair flying, spinning, bouncing, upside down, sideways. The music throbbed and so did Taggart's cock as he watched her tits and ass and spreading legs. She finished with her backwards handstand dismount from the pole and then threw her hands in the air in front of Taggart. He clapped and she frowned.

"What?" Taggart asked, a confused look on his face.

"You didn't like it, did you?"

"Are you crazy? I thought it was awesome."

"I don't believe you."

"Want me to show you?"

She smiled and nodded vigorously.

Taggart stood up and dropped his drawers and underwear to his ankles, his cock pointing straight out towards her.

"You did like it!" she exclaimed and clapped. She eyed his rigid member like a hungry panther. "I want to dance on that pole."

"Get on it then!"

After licking and sucking her sweet peach of a pussy and bringing her to multiple orgasms, he picked her up off the futon and laid her on the grain colored carpet of the living room. He was about to slip into between her legs but she stopped him. "You have to be on bottom. I have a competition in a week and can't have any rug burns."

Taggart rolled over onto his back and Stacy stood with her feet at his sides and then squatted over his cock as if she were about to take a shit, but then slipped her pussy over his shaft as if sheathing a knife. Her hot, wet pussy engulfed him and he lifted his hips to meet her as her ass cheeks smacked down upon his thighs. He reached for her tits and she leaned forward and grasped onto his arms for balance while her hips raised and lowered and his throbbing cock appeared and disappeared over and over again into her fiery bush.

The music pounded through the trailer as their bodies pounded together. Stacy screamed in delight as Taggart

46

pinched her stiff nipples while his ass bounced off the floor faster and faster, his cock ramming in and out of her until she was panting and screaming and digging her nails into his forearms.

Taggart let loose with a roar as his cock let loose with a flood of his hot man juice deep within Stacy's spasming, jerking body until she collapsed upon his chest as worn out as she'd ever been while working any pole.

Before he left Stacy made them another drink and he let her hold his gun. Taggart took her number and promised he'd be back sometime for more pole action, a promise he thought he might even keep.

On the way to the county medical center the chief called and told him the counterfeit hundred dollar bills had shown up in Texas. He was to make arrangements to get there immediately. Taggart liked the thought of that because he'd heard good things about the strip clubs in Texas.

Part 3

I See You

I

Croak didn't like women with no meat on their bones and who had fake tits, acrylic nails, pasted on eyelashes, hair extensions and too much make up painted on their faces. That was only one of a hundred reasons why he hated Las Vegas. And now that he was laying in Clark County Medical Center ICU with a gunshot wound to his shoulder, his body battered and bruised by police and security personnel, and a police detail outside his room, he had even more reason to hate this god forsaken city in the desert.

"What's the matter? Don't you like?" Juanita asked.

"I was just thinking," Croak said. "Don't stop."

Juanita Calle was an all natural woman, all two hundred and eighty pleasantly plump pounds of her. She stood beside Croak's hospital bed with her back to the door and curtained monitored window, her body blocking her actions from anyone who might peek in. She had worked at CCMC for seventeen months and was wearing her standard RN uniform of white shoes, white pants, and white buttoned up shirt with her name tag on the pocket.

"Slower," Croak said.

"Slower?"

"That's what I said," he growled.

Juanita's right hand slowed down beneath the covers of the bed where it was stroking the injured man's rigid cock. She had been jacking him off for almost ten minutes now and was becoming more and more worried that another nurse or orderly might check up on her.

"That's it, right there. Long, slow, smooth strokes."

"We need to hurry."

"You need to do what you're paid to do. Come here." Croak raised his right hand that was handcuffed to the bed just as his left hand was handcuffed to the other side of the bed. With a concerned look she moved closer to the head of the bed, pushing up next to the IV stand and computer that monitored the patient's vitals. Her hand continued sliding up and down his cock. "Take out a titty."

Juanita's eyes grew wide and she shook her head. She swallowed and her throat felt constricted as she spoke in a whisper. "That is no good."

Croak's dead gray eyes squinted through back slits and she was sure his voice was just what the devil's would sound like. "Don't you tell me no. Your brother has already been paid

48

the ten grand for you to take care of whatever I say. Did he tell you that?" Juanita nodded. "If you do not comply, the money will disappear and so will your baby brother. Now give me your tit and don't stop stroking."

Juanita's younger brother had been involved in some things he shouldn't be in the Green Triangle in the upper northwest but he excused his actions because he said he was doing it to make money so all the relatives could come to the United States from Mexico. "If we do this job for Croak, he pays us ten before and ten when it's done and we'll get to see mama and papa and Aunt Lucinda," Paco had told her.

"What is this name, Croak?" Juanita asked. "Isn't that a sound a frog makes?"

"Or it means death," her little brother told her over the phone.

A chill ran through her body but she said she would do it, whatever it takes to see all her family together once again.

With her left hand she began to unbutton the top of her shirt while her right hand continued moving over his veiny member. She kept her eyes on her left hand, not wanting to see what her right hand was doing and not wanting to look into Croak's cold eyes. When her shirt was half way unbuttoned she pulled it aside to expose her white Walmart bra. She pulled the bra down, baring her brown skinned breast and then bent over so Croak could reach it with his restrained hand.

She had a dark brown nipple like a Hershey's Kiss and Croak twisted it back and forth in his fingers like it was a radio dial. "You like that, don't you?" he said and Juanita nodded, still not looking at him. His strong, bony hand clasped her large, fleshy breast, his fingers digging into her painfully. She felt him become even harder in her right hand and she began to jerk it faster per his command.

Croak squeezed her tit harder and she bit her lip to keep from crying out. His thighs tensed and his ass clenched as he felt the volcano surging in his loins and rising up through his cock and then he was exploding his hot lava into the sheets, onto his belly, all over Juanita's hand. "Milk it," he told her. "Oh

49

yeah, get it all." His right hand released her boob, leaving bruise marks, and dropped back to the bed like a dead fish. She covered herself and rebuttoned her shirt with her left hand.

"That is good?" she asked as his cock became limp in her cramped hand.

"Yeah. Clean me up."

Juanita quickly went to the adjoining bathroom and ran a towel under the hot water while washing her hand. She returned to the bedside to clean croak's sticky mess and change the cover sheet.

"You make sure the nurse's station is empty at exactly two fifteen," Croak said.

"Yes, I know." She left the room without looking back at the evil man.

II

It was less than two hours until patrol officer Paulson was off duty and would be relieved of his boring babysitting detail. He knew the chief was punishing him simply because he'd accidentally sideswiped a brand new Lamborghini on the strip. Wasn't that what insurance was for? Nonetheless, he was pretty certain he'd be back on regular patrol by next week.

Officer Paulson was struggling with a Sudoku puzzle book and didn't hear the Code Red that pulled all the nurses and doctors away from the nurse's station fifteen feet away. He also paid no mind to the black orderly who was pushing a gurney toward him down the hallway. Paulson was debating whether to write a 3 or a 4 in an empty space on the eighty-one square grid when he caught a quick motion out of the corner of his eye. He looked up in time to catch the metal frame of the gurney being rammed into his throat and bashing the back of his head into the wall, causing an indent in the plaster. The patrolman fell off his chair unconscious, air struggling to get through his crushed trachea.

Smoothly and efficiently BC opened the ICU door to Croak's room and shoved the gurney in and then he grabbed the patrolman by the collar and dragged his body into the room. He shut the door behind him.

"You're looking fresh and chipper," BC said to his longtime friend and partner.

"The nurses have been taking good care of me," Croak replied.

"I bet," the giant black man said as he approached the hospital bed with a handcuff key in his hand.

As soon as his hands were free Croak went to pull the IV from his right arm with his left, but the pain in his shoulder was too much. "Pull this shit out of my arm!" he told BC. BC did so and helped steady him as he got out of the bed and walked the few steps to the gurney. Croak bent down and pulled out the officer's service handgun, putting it in his lap under the gurney's covers.

"Find my poncho," Croak said just as BC was about to open the door.

"You can get another one."

"Find it!"

BC found all of Croak's clothes, most covered in blood, in a bag in the room's only closet. He tossed it on the gurney and then quickly pushed him out of the room. BC retraced his path with the gurney to an elevator at the far end of the hall. He pushed the button and when the metal door slid open he pushed the gurney inside.

"Whoa, whoa, whoa!" a small, balding doctor said, stopping the gurney half in the elevator car. "What are you doing? This is an employee only elevator. What's your name?"

The big, bulky black man known as Boxcar since sixth grade looked from the irate doctor to the small name tag on his chest and then back to the doctor. "I'm Liebowitz," BC told him.

"You're who?" the doctor asked, stepping beside the gurney and approaching BC as if the doctor were god himself. "I'll have you cleaning bed pans for a week. Now get this thing out of here!"

BC was almost a foot taller than the doctor and twice as heavy and he leaned down, pointing to his broad, black forehead and said, "Look at this." He said it so softly the doctor barely heard him but he looked to where BC was pointing. BC's forehead smashed into the doctor's face and the doc dropped to the floor of the elevator like a marionette whose strings had been cut.

Three minutes later BC and Croak were out of the hospital and in a black GMC Yukon Denali driven by a sexy little Asian lady.

"Croak, Kiki. Kiki, Croak," BC said making the introductions.

"Hang on, bitches!" Kiki said as she tore out of the hospital lot.

III

Croak was floating on a pain free Oxycontin drug induced heat wave hotter than the desert. Not the dirty, barren, ugly sands of Las Vegas but rather the lush vibrancy of an African savannah like a yellow banana where he was king, a lion with a dreadlock mane hunting the plain and feeling no pain. He heard the cackle of a jackal that raised his hackles and his eyes opened a slit to reveal a blurry, run down motel room. The high pitched laughter he heard came from the other side of the wall behind him where BC and Kiki were. Croak closed his eyes and returned to the fields of gold where he never felt cold and he roamed wild and bold. He heard the jackal's laughter again and this time he saw her on all fours near a line of trees. She stood on hind legs exposing her huge fake breasts and bare pussy; the king of the jungle turned away looking for something with more meat on its bones. He heard the trumpeting of an elephant and Croak's eyes barely opened again in the motel room. The sound repeated itself, a man blowing his nose in the adjoining room behind the paper thin wall. Croak closed his eyes and the lion ran free through the soothing heat ignoring the jackals and elephants.

"It's like an elephant trunk," Kiki said as she stood before the naked black man and looking at the almost thirteen inches of meat swinging between his legs. She grasped it in both hands and raised it in the air making an elephant sound that then turned to laughter. BC smiled, not so much at the joke but merely because she was handling his cock.

Kiki stood before him in all her naked glory, the top of her head barely reaching to BC's chest. She held the head of his penis in one hand while sliding her other hand up the length of his shaft, feeling all of the ridges and veins. "It's like a big boa constrictor," the small Asian said looking up at him with a smile.

"Or a lollipop," he replied smiling down at her.

"Oh, I see what you're getting at," she said shaking a finger at him. Kiki then grasped the middle of his cock as she would if holding a huge cheeseburger and she opened her mouth wide. The tip of his big, black penis brushed against her lips and for a brief moment she didn't think it was going to fit but then her mouth was full of him. She'd seen and handled a lot of cocks in her profession, but his was by far the longest and thickest. She was excited at the challenge it represented.

The two of them were standing in front of the foot of the bed, Kiki squatting as if sitting in an invisible chair as she slathered the tip of his cock with saliva moving her head back and forth.

"There you go, girl," BC said as the room filled with her slurping sounds. Lines of spittle dripped from his cock which Kiki caught in her hand and used for lube as she twisted her hands back and forth the length of his shaft. "Work it, work it," BC told her as he soaked in the sensations.

After ten or fifteen minutes of her manhandling, BC scooped her up by her armpits and tossed her onto the bed. He straddled the side of the bed, one foot on the floor and his knee on the bed, and then grabbed Kiki's hips and pulled her toward

53

him. She liked how he took control and how easily he flipped her around.

"Ohhhhh!" she said as she spread her legs and he pushed his cock into her. Kiki had never felt so full in her life. After six inches she though he was pushing against her inner organs, and after seven she thought he was going to push them up through her throat. Eight was all she could take and she cried mercy. BC was impressed she could take as much of him as she did and he proceeded to fuck her with as much as she could handle. He'd become accustomed to not being able to fully penetrate women.

"Give me your thumb," Kiki told him as he thrust in and out of her, her large tits bouncing back and forth. She took his offered right hand and stuck his thumb into her mouth, sucking on it and slathering it with her spit like she'd done with the head of his cock. "Stick it in my ass," she told him.

BC slipped his spit-lubed thumb into her tight little asshole, sliding it in and out of her while his cock did the same. The big man's thumb was larger than many of the Asian cocks she's had, and some white guys for that matter, and Kiki was crying out, "Yeah yeah oh yeah!" over and over again as orgasms rippled through her body like multiple tornado touchdowns.

BC was oh-yeahing with her as he neared completion and Kiki was telling him, "Pull it out! Give it to me! Whitewash me!"

He yanked his cock out and pulled his thumb out of Kiki's ass, gripping his cock and stroking it vigorously until his milky white cream was shooting forth. The hot jizz covered her torso, shot between her tits, and splashed against her chin as he groaned like a grizzly. Kiki's hands clasped onto his cock, stroking and milking him of every last drop.

"That was fun!" Kiki said as he went to the bathroom to wash his hands.

He stepped out of the bathroom with a towel. "Need this?"

"Not yet," she said as she slathered his cum all over her body as if it were lotion. BC figured she was bat shit crazy, but what did he care? She was sexy as fuck. "We need to find you a horse pussy," Kiki said as he sat on the bed next to her.

"I ain't into no bestiality."

"Not a horse, silly. A woman with a horse pussy so you can ram all the way into her."

BC smiled and nodded. Yep, bat shit crazy, he thought.

"Where does one find a woman with a horse pussy?" he asked.

"We're in Vegas, baby!" Kiki laughed. "It has everything!"

IV

An hour later Missy had joined them in the room. She was almost six feet tall with dark, wavy brown hair that fell to her medium sized boobs. She had thick thighs, a big booty and was half Puerto Rican, half Russian and had thirteen inches of African American in her. BC had her bent over the side of the bed with his hands clasped to her hips as he rammed his cock into her, his pelvis bouncing off her quivering thighs. The look on Misty's face was pure bliss and she accompanied each thrust with Russian swear words.

Kiki was propped up at the head of the bed watching the two fuck while she pleased herself with a large chrome vibrator. She had tried kissing on Missy and playing with her tits but the tall lady was adamantly not interested in what she called "lezbo action." Kiki looked at BC who seemed to be in heaven, his head arched back as his hips rocked back and forth, the slapping of flesh and Russian cries filling the small room.

It had been a long time since BC had been able to grind his groin against the cushion of a woman's ass cheeks while his cock sunk all the way into her. It felt so good to have every inch of his rigid member in her deep, warm wetness and he didn't ever want to stop. Of course, it had helped that Kiki had gotten him off earlier and now twenty minutes later he was still thrusting away.

"On the bed," Missy gasped. "My legs, I can't stand." BC and Missy moved onto the bed on their sides and Kiki spread her legs to make space for them. "Get your twat out of my face," Missy told her.

"Put it in mine," BC said and Kiki smiled ear to ear as she tossed the vibrator aside and scooted her bare pussy against BC's mouth. He nuzzled his big lips against her small lips and proceeded to lick and suck while fucking Missy sideways from behind. Despite her propensity for taking big cock, Missy could never orgasm from intercourse alone so she licked the fingers of one hand and began stimulating her clit. Soon all three were moaning and grunting in delight.

The motel door opened and Croak stood there in his poncho observing the threesome. "What is this, the league of nations?" he asked.

"You come too!" Kiki called out from the bed.

"No," he said and looked at BC. "Finish up. We have work to do." With that Croak walked away and the motel door closed.

Five minutes later BC's cock was exploding inside Missy and Kiki had her arms wrapped around BC's bald head as her pussy spasmed against his mouth. The trio slowly disentangled and got dressed. Missy was paid for her services and left while BC and Kiki went next door to get Croak.

V

Stacy was practicing for the upcoming pole dancing competition that was only days away. She was topless and wearing a white thong that stood out on her lithe tan body and fiery red hair. Disturbed boomed through the speakers as she grabbed the pole in her living room up high and then slid one leg up the pole while her other flattened against the lower portion of the pole and she was doing the vertical splits.

The screen door to the double wide trailer opened and Stacy dipped her head back to see two upside down figures stepping into her home. She straightened herself and hopped off the pole to confront the tall thin white guy and even taller huge black guy. "Um, can I help you?"

The white guy had a look of pain on his face, like he was in it and like he could give it. He ignored her and began walking to the back of the trailer.

"Hey!" Stacy yelled at him.

The screen door opened again and Kiki stepped into the trailer. When Stacy saw her the fear and concern on her face became less pronounced and the tension building in her shoulders eased.

"Hi, Kiki. What's going on?"

"They looking for Fantasia. What you doing?"

"Training for this weekend."

"You looking good," Kiki said, eyeing her up and down. She'd always tried to get into Stacy's pants but Stacy didn't freak that way. Now when she saw her it was just playful flirting.

"Thanks," Stacy said blushing slightly. She looked at the big black guy who hadn't moved from next to the doorway, hadn't said anything, and who was looking at her but not really looking at her. She could hear the other guy rummaging through the back room of the trailer. "I haven't seen her in a few days. I heard she might be in some trouble."

"Where you hear that?" Kiki asked.

"There was an agent here asking questions this morning."

"What agent?" Croak asked as he returned from the back of the trailer. He held a small, green address book in his hands.

"He was from the Treasury Department," Stacy said, suddenly feeling cold in only her thong and the icy eyes of the white guy on her. "He left his card," she said and walked toward the kitchen counter as Croak did the same. She handed him Agent Taggart's card.

Croak looked at the card and then looked at BC. "Get the computer," he told him and BC exited the trailer, having to duck his head through the doorway as he did so. To Stacy he said, "Have a seat," and motioned toward the brown futon. "What did you tell this Agent Taggart?"

Kiki was hanging onto the stripper pole with one hand and lazily swinging around in slow circles. She had never been a stripper and had never done anything but play around on a pole. Disturbed had moved onto the next song on their album, and though Croak's voice was low, it cut through the music effortlessly. He watched the petite redhead intently.

"I didn't tell him anything," Stacy said. "I didn't know anything about any trouble. I haven't seen her since Sunday or Monday. Besides, I told him that Renae isn't the type of girl to get in trouble."

"She's a whore, isn't she?" Croak asked coldly.

"No, she's an escort," Stacy said defensively.

"What's the difference?"

"It's legal in Vegas," Kiki piped up from the pole.

"That doesn't change the terminology," Croak said. "Whatever you want to call it, she sells her ass."

"But that doesn't mean she gets into trouble," Stacy said, still defending her roommate.

"She had no problem spending stolen money," Croak said. "Money stolen from me."

"Do you have wifi?" BC asked. Stacy told him the network name and the password and BC tapped away on his little computer.

"I've tried calling her, but her phone is de--" Stacy caught herself from saying a word she didn't want to associate with Renae. "Her phone's off."

"Yes, we know. Back to the Treasury agent," Croak said. "What did he say about her or her whereabouts?"

Stacy wasn't about to tell him that the agent's visit ended up being more about fucking her than talking about her roommate. "He didn't know anything about her, that's why he was asking questions."

"Where's your phone?" Croak asked. She pointed to an end table and Kiki grabbed it and handed it to her. "In a minute I want you to call this Agent Taggart and ask him if he's found out anything about Renae's whereabouts. And don't say anything about us."

Stacy nodded her head.

Croak looked to BC. BC nodded.

Croak turned back and nodded at Stacy.

Kiki was nodding her head to the heavy rock music.

Croak sat down on the futon next to Stacy and held the agent's card while she looked at it and punched the numbers into her phone. It rang twice and was answered.

"Taggart here."

"Hi, this is Stacy."

There was silence on the other end of the line. Croak mouthed 'speakerphone' and Stacy tapped a button.

"You, um, interviewed me yesterday."

"Of course. How's the pole practice coming along?"

Stacy smiled at the thought of practicing on his pole. "It's good. I was wondering if you found out anything about Renae."

"I can't discuss an ongoing investigation."

"She's my friend. I just want to know that she's okay."

"I understand. I'm following up on a lead right now. How about this? If she calls or shows up, you promise not to tell her about me, and you call me right away. She's mixed up with some bad people, very dangerous. I'm trying to save her. As soon as I have her safely in custody I promise to call you. I'd like to see you again."

"Okay," Stacy said. "I'd like that a lot."

"Bye for now."

"Bye."

Croak looked toward BC who gave him a gold toothed smile. "Ever been to Dallas?" BC asked.

Croak put Agent Taggart's card into his shirt pocket beneath his poncho. With his left hand he gritted through the pain as he reached for a throw pillow on the futon and handed it to Stacy. It was almost too heavy to hold. "Cover yourself," he told her and looked at her pink tipped breasts.

Stacy's brow crinkled in confusion as she slowly pressed the golden fringed red pillow over her chest.

Croak's right hand came out from beneath his poncho holding the stolen patrolman's .40 Smith and Wesson handgun. In one swift motion he pressed the barrel against the pillow and fired one shot into her heart.

Though somewhat muffled by the pillow, the gunshot was still loud within the trailer. The loud music of Disturbed drowned out enough of the sound outside the mobile home to not draw any attention.

Kiki screamed and slipped from the pole, falling to her ass on the carpeted floor. Her eyes and mouth were all small O's.

"Did you touch anything?" Croak asked BC.

"Just the screen door," the big man replied as he scooped up his computer.

"Wipe it down and let's hit the road," Croak said as he stood up from the futon, the gun hanging down at his side. He turned and looked at Kiki.

The small Asian lady in the sea foam green thigh high dress with double straps over her shoulder sat in stunned silence looking at the dead woman on the futon. Stacy's unblinking eyes were open in an expression of 'could-this-really-be-happening.'

"Kiki." It was BC's deep, low voice.

Kiki looked away from Stacy and up at Croak. "Why you do that?"

"Are you coming or staying?" Croak asked simply. Kiki was pretty sure she knew what he meant by staying. Her only option was to ride with Croak and BC until she could find a time to escape safely. She didn't want to die.

"I'm coming."

Part 4

Doing It In Dallas

I

"I'm coming!" Renae screamed out. "Oh fuck, I'm coming!"

"Yes!" Duncan grunted from beneath her, his hips bucking wildly, his hands clasped to her ass as she rode him like a rodeo bronco.

Renae's nails dug into his sweat glistened chest and she whipped her head from side to side as Duncan's cock plunged in and out of her wet, warm pussy. "Oh, don't stop," she said as her body quivered and orgasmed again and again. Duncan kept bouncing his ass off the motel bed not wanting to ever stop as his cock rose up and down sheathed in her tight hole.

As if someone had pushed the fast forward button on Duncan's pelvis, the tempo increased rapidly, their flesh smacking together like hands clapping and then both of them were crying out in unison as Duncan's milky load filled the reservoir tip of his condom.

"Oh god, I needed that," Renae said as she laid her breasts upon Duncan's chest, both their bodies slick with sweat. His breathing was heavy as she settled her head against his shoulder. He let his hands roam up and down her back, in her ass crack, over her thighs. She let her fingers play in his sandy brown hair and then stretched her legs straight so she was laying completely atop Duncan.

They laid there together for some time, their hearts thumping back and forth within their chests, their bodies touching at all points. Duncan's deflated member still cozied inside Renae.

"Are you hot?" Renae asked him.

"Not as hot as you," he replied.

"Funny." She looked over at the battered air conditioner and heating unit attached to the wall beneath the curtained window. When they had begun their sexcapades the unit had been rattling and spewing cool air into the room but now it sat dead. From outside the room traffic could be heard roaring nonstop from the freeway in front of their motel.

Renae rolled off the top of Duncan, his limp dick plopping out of her like a sad worm, and she scooted off the bed to the air conditioner. Duncan's fingers meandered at his balls, playing with them as he watched the naked beauty bent over fiddling with the buttons of the AC. Goddamn, Duncan thought, she had the most beautiful ass he'd ever seen, perfectly shaped, tight, toned and tan - he could live in that thing for days. His penis tingled but didn't come back to life yet.

"It might be broken," Renae said, looking at Duncan.

"No, I just need a little more time," he told her.

"I'm talking about the air conditioner."

"Oh." He smiled sheepishly.

She smiled and shook her head. "Come on, let's get out of here."

"Did we forget something?" Duncan asked and looked around at the half a dozen shopping bags from different clothing stores scattered about the room. In their haste to leave Las Vegas, the only thing they had left with was the trunk full of counterfeit cash. They had purchased food and necessities while on the road and then went on a spending spree once they reached Dallas.

"There's something I've always wanted to do," Renae said.

"If you want to do it, I want to do it," Duncan told her.

She moved to the side of the bed and kissed him. "See, that's why we get along so well." She slipped the partially full condom from his dick and then flicked his wilted member with her finger. "Of course, if this guy doesn't come back to life you're no good to me."

Duncan's eyes darted to hers. Renae laughed and said, "I'm kidding."

II

"Are you serious?" Duncan asked.

"He was standing right here when he was shot," Renae said.

The two of them were standing on a sidewalk in front of a large red brick building with many windows. The sun beat down on them through a clear blue sky, Duncan in a pair of brown Dockers and a white Polo shirt while Renae wore a short, flowing summer dress with squiggly blue, green and yellow designs all over. She had her left hand over her eyes for a sun visor and pointed across Dailey Plaza with her right hand.

"President Kennedy was about there when the first shot was fired," Renae said, "and my dad was standing right here. Can you imagine?"

Duncan didn't have to imagine. He could see the black and white reel playing in his mind reliving the moment when the president's head jerked back from the impact of the rifle round, a piece of his skull landing on the trunk of the black, Lincoln convertible, Jackie Kennedy frantically reaching from the backseat to grab the piece of her husband's skull from atop the trunk, the motorcade speeding off amid shouts, screams and sirens.

"My dad was looking over there," Renae said as she directed her arm across the other side of the plaza. "That was the grassy knoll where people had thought they heard the shots come from. My dad said he had even seen a puff of smoke from that direction."

"Isn't that the conspiracy theory?" Duncan asked. He looked up at the Texas School Book Depository building that they were standing in front of. It was one of the fifth floor windows on the right that Lee Harvey Oswald was said to have fired his rifle from. "So your dad didn't believe Oswald did it?"

Renae looked at Duncan. "Oh my dad knew Lee did it. He even bumped into my dad coming out of this building. Lee mumbled excuse me and disappeared around the corner but my dad was focused on all the commotion, cops everywhere. It wasn't until later that night that my dad realized that the assassin had bumped him while making his escape. My dad was only fifteen at the time."

"Wow, that's crazy," Duncan said.

"It gets crazier. My dad finishes high school, joins the army and fights in Vietnam and returns to this spot on the ten year anniversary of the shooting. That's when he meets my mother, right here in this same spot. She's a senior in high school on a field trip with her class from Las Vegas and my dad falls instantly, madly in love. Emphasis on the madly part. He follows her to Vegas and they get married as soon as she graduates and nine months later I'm brought into the world."

"Wait. So you were born in Las Vegas? I thought you said you'd only been there for a couple years."

Renae smiled and touched his arm. She liked that he actually listened and paid attention to her because she had told him during their drive through the desert that she'd only been in Vegas for a couple of years. "I lived there until I was eleven," she said. "My parents fought all the time. The war had messed up my dad's head and he'd wake up screaming from nightmares and sometimes even have flashbacks during the day. I returned home from school one day to find him digging a foxhole in the backyard and when he sees me he begins yelling at me to get down, take cover, as he's lifting up a rifle to his shoulder. I ran into the house screaming, my dad's in the backyard screaming, and then my mom's screaming and I don't know if it's at me or my dad. And he was super jealous and possessive of my mom which was a huge problem because she worked as a showgirl at Maxim Hotel and Casino. I used to love seeing her in her costume and she'd show me some of her routines, but I never got to see her live on stage because my dad refused to take me there. He used to say he was going to bomb the casino."

Renae took Duncan's hand and said, "Let's get out of this sun." They walked back toward the parking garage a few blocks away.

III

"So you guys moved from Las Vegas when you were eleven?" Duncan asked.

"Ooh, over there!" Renae said and pulled Duncan across the street to an ice cream shop called Cherry on Top. They each got cones with double scoops and walked outside with tongues in full licking action. They smiled at each other as both had pleasantly naughty thoughts watching the other's tongue.

"Okay, I want to hear the rest," Duncan said. "You and your folks left Vegas."

Renae shook her head. Duncan watched her lick some strawberry ice cream from her bottom lip before she said, "No, just me. My parents were dead."

"Whoa. Wait. What?"

"It was termed a murder-suicide," Renae said and took some licks of her ice cream cone, the first scoop almost gone. "But I was upstairs when I heard the first shot. I snuck downstairs and peeked around the corner into the kitchen and there my dad was, sitting on the yellow and white tiled floor, leaned up against the chipped and flaked green steel cabinet doors, both his hands clutching his bloody stomach. 'That's what you get!' my mother was screaming at him, holding his M1 rifle at her waist and approaching him, screaming and crying and my dad was crying and then I knew she was too close, I was going to tell her she was too close but it was too late and they didn't know I was there.

"He grabbed the rifle and they both struggled, she was yanking him across the kitchen floor leaving a bloody, red

65

smear behind him, both of them screaming and crying until the rifle went off and every sound in the world stopped. My mother's face exploded like a dropped tomato and she fell to the floor, and the gun fell to the floor, and my dad fell to the floor. I saw all this like watching a slow motion movie with no sound. My eardrums were blown from the rifle's explosion within the kitchen and it was over a week until I could hear again."

Duncan and Renae had reached the entrance of the parking garage, though Duncan was so entranced in her story he'd forgotten all about his ice cream cone and it had melted down all sides of his hand.

"How could that be termed a murder suicide?" he asked.

"I went catatonic, didn't speak for almost a year. I was sent to my mother's older sister who was living in southern Georgia. When I finally told my grandmother what had really happened she said it didn't change the end result none and to just leave it be. I went to college and hated every minute of the academics but loved the partying and sex. I managed to graduate only because a couple of the professors let me earn extra credit outside of the classroom. Let me say this: it fucking rocks to be a beautiful girl in America - I can get anything I want. Anything at all."

They were alone in the parking ramp elevator on the way to the fourth floor when Renae motioned to Duncan's melted cone in his hand. She had finished her's. "Can I have that?" she asked.

Duncan handed her the cone and its melted swirl of chocolate and vanilla in the middle. "Pull out your cock and dip it in here so I can lick it off," Renae told him. He was unzipping his pants before she finished the sentence. "And when we get to the car will you eat out my pussy on the hood of the car until I orgasm?"

"Absolutely," Duncan said happily as he slipped his semi hard cock out of his zipper.

"See, it just proves my point. I can get anything I want." Renae grabbed his penis and dipped it fully into the mushy ice cream cone. Duncan wasn't about to argue her point, he was merely thrilled that what she wanted was him.

IV

The elevator dinged and the metal doors slid open on the fourth floor. Two old ladies in conservative dresses and big floppy sun hats stood in the doorway waiting to get on. One of the ladies gasped when she saw Renae holding Duncan's penis in the ice cream cone, chocolate and vanilla dripping out the sides.

"Well I never!" one of the old ladies said as Renae led Duncan out of the elevator by his man rope.

"Don't knock it 'til you try it, lady," Renae said as the elevator doors closed on the old ladies' gaping mouths. Renae gaped her own mouth and took Duncan's cold, ice cream covered cock into it. The warmth of her mouth counteracted the cold and brought him quickly to life. They heard a car door slam not too far away in the parking garage and Renae took a couple more licks of his flavorful cock before slipping him out of her mouth. He was about to tuck himself back into his pants but she said, "No, leave it." Once again, he knew this was not something he wanted to argue. She led him behind a white Chevy Tahoe as they heard heavy footsteps pass them by on the way to the elevator.

Renae crouched down and wrapped her luscious lips around the head of Duncan's cock and slowly took him into her mouth, her lips sliding over every veiny ridge until her chin was brushing against his balls.

"Holy fuck yeah," Duncan moaned as she moved her mouth back and forth the length of his shaft. Her tongue swirled around the bulbous purple tip of his cock as if it were one of the ice cream scoops she had just devoured. Duncan looked down at her doing her magic and realize this was the first time she had taken him without putting a condom on him. And it felt fucking amazing.

He became lost in the sensations of her mouth and lips and tongue, as well as her hands twisting and stroking the base of his cock. He heard an occasional car or footsteps and the dinging of the elevator but none if it mattered as he stood glued to his spot and she worked his raging hard on to perfection. Renae's lips slurped up and down, her fingers squeezed and jerked back and forth, everything moving faster, harder.

Duncan felt it coming, his legs trembling, his ass cheeks clenching. He plastered one of his dirty, sticky hands on the back window of the Tahoe to brace himself. Renae's head bobbed back and forth vigorously as he fucked her mouth and then he was graoning as his hot juices shot into her throat. She sucked and swallowed as he spurted more and she continued to milk him dry. She gave his cock one last good cleaning with her tongue before slipping him back into his pants and zipping him up.

"I think I need to sit down," Duncan said, his legs feeling weak.

"Oh no you don't," Renae told him. "You still have work to do."

V

"You're something amazing," he told her as they walked to his maroon Mustang parked in a far corner. He slipped his hands under her armpits and helped her to sit on the hood of his car, the metal warm beneath her bare thighs. "So how did you end up back in Vegas doing what you do?"

"I'm not saying another word until you give me what you promised," she said with a smile.

"Don't threaten me with a good time," Duncan replied. He grabbed her knees and spread them apart and then lifted up her sundress. Her pussy was bare and glistening, eagerly awaiting him. He slid his tongue down the inside of her thigh until he reached her honey pot. Deeply he breathed in the scent of her sex, her sweat, her fragrant perfume, and ice cream. He put his mouth upon her and slowly gyrated his entire head as he applied soft pressure to her vulva.

"Ooh, I like that," Renae cooed. A pickup truck rolled by but Duncan didn't see it and Renae didn't care who was in it. "He's just checking my oil," she said flippantly over her shoulder as the vehicle continued on down the parking garage.

Renae flipped off her sandals so her feet would stop slipping off the hood of the car. One of Duncan's hands was gripping one of her ass cheeks while two fingers of the other hand were gently sliding in and out of her wet pussy. His lips and tongue continued nuzzling, licking, sucking.

"Okay, yeah," she said in a dreamy voice. "After college I went to Vegas to be a showgirl but I had no idea of the fierce competition I'd have. I didn't have any serious dancing background whereas some of these girls have been in dance classes - jazz, ballet, tap - since they were like five years old. Ooh, ooh, yeah, right there, baby."

Renae curled her fingers in Duncan's hair and grinded his face into her pussy, his tongue wet and warm against her. His fingers twisted and turned inside her and then she felt his thumb rubbing against her anus. She spread her legs wider and leaned back and then sucked in her breath when his saliva slathered thumb pushed inside her.

"Oh yes. That. Where was I?" Her whole body was rocking like a small wave. "So I started dancing at a strip club, figured that would be a stepping stone to the showgirl stage. But I realized at the club that practically every guy wanted to take me home, or rather back to their hotel room. I'm not ashamed to admit I was kind of a slut back in high school and college - what can I say, I love sex. Oh my god, yes, right there just like that, don't stop. Oh god yes, oh god yes, oh god yes!"

The Mustang was rocking back and forth as Renae clung to Duncan's head that continued grinding against and gratifying her pulsating pussy. His hand was shaking back and forth with fingers in her pussy and a thumb in her ass. His other hand slid up her dress and was squeezing her breast and pinching the nipple between his fingers. Renae's thighs and legs were quivering and her pelvis was jerking against Duncan's face as orgasms spiraled out of control in every direction. She howled like a coyote that echoed throughout the parking garage. On one of the floors a car alarm went off.

VI

As they drove back to the motel, Renae sat in the passenger's seat softly stroking Duncan's cock what was tall and stiff sticking out of his pants. "I love that you get hard when you eat me out," she said as she looked at him and smiled. "We're going to put this to good use when we get back."

"Did you finish your story?" he asked her.

"Pretty much. I took my grandma's advice and decided to start getting paid for what I love to do."

"Does your grandma know what you do?"

"No, that grandma died when I was fifteen. My only other relative is my aunt in Georgia and she knows everything."

"Really? And she's okay with it, with what you do?"

"Yeah. What's the big deal? Do you have a problem with what I do?"

Duncan looked at her and said, "I don't have a problem with what you do," and then looked down at her hand stroking his cock, "or what you're doing. And you do it so well."

"Thank you."

As they pulled into the motel parking lot Renae asked, "Do you think we're still in danger?"

Duncan shook his head. "No. After that debacle in Vegas I'm sure Croak is either dead or in jail."

"I just hope Kiki's okay."

"Yeah, she's still not on my favorite person list."

"She didn't mean you any harm."

"I've still got a lump on my head that proves otherwise," Duncan said. "And even if she didn't want to hurt me, she did want to steal all my money."

"Your money?"

"It is now," he said as he parked in front of their motel room.

"I'm sorry, I didn't mean to get you upset," Renae said as she held his limp dick in her hand. "Let's go inside and fix this."

Once again Duncan could find no reason to argue.

As they walked into the motel room Renae said, "My roommate Stacy was telling me about Dallas having the biggest strip club in the nation. Maybe later tonight we can go."

Part 5

Busted

I

"Do you want to go?" agent Kevin Michaels asked agent Gary Taggart as they stood in the Dallas office of the U.S. Treasury. Other agents in the office were donning ballistic vests and checking weapons, the excitement and adrenaline wafting from their bodies as pungent as the perfume counter at Macy's.

Taggart had arrived at the justice building only thirty minutes prior, having taken a taxi from Dallas his hotel. Michaels had been expecting him; he'd heard Taggart's name from a mutual friend in the agency before said friend was killed in the line of duty less than a year ago. When Taggart and

Michaels met it was evident they could almost be brothers. Both men were in their mid thirties, around six feet tall, blue eyes (though Michaels' were a bit more hazel), and toned bodies from regular sessions in the gym. Both men were even wearing blue jeans, black running shoes, and button up short sleeved shirts, though Taggart's was yellow and brown earth tones whereas Michaels' was black and green striped. The only significant difference between the men was Taggart's bald head and Michaels' brown crew cut.

"Where are we going?" Taggart asked.

"Hey Lou, grab me an extra vest," Michaels yelled to an agent across the office. To Taggart he said, "A CI gave us a warehouse where they've been printing money. A lot of it. And we know it's there right now."

The other agent tossed a ballistic vest to Taggart and he slipped it on. Bold yellow lettering on the back read: U.S. Treasury. He followed Michaels and half a dozen other agents out of the office and to four unmarked government vehicles.

As Taggart rode with Michaels, the Dallas based agent asked him, "How do you feel about porn?"

The question came out of left field and caught Taggart by surprise. He wondered if this were some sort of test or trick question. He looked over skeptically at the driver and said, "Like it?"

Michaels smiled and said, "Then you'll like this bust."

II

"I'm gonna bust! I'm gonna bust!" the big titted woman cried out. She was laying on her back on large, plastic wrapped bundles of hundred dollar bills that were stacked up over three feet high in the middle of a bank vault. A white button up shirt that had been torn away from her body draped down one side of the bed of money, along with her tattered black bra and her very large, surgically enhanced breasts defied gravity as they

72

jiggled back and forth. A gold plated name tag could be seen pinned to her useless shirt. It read: Holly, Head Teller.

The black pinstripe skirt Holly had been wearing was in a heap on the vault floor along with a pair of white lace panties that looked like they had been torn off her voluptuous hips. Holly still wore her dangerously tall black stiletto heels but they were waving useless in the air.

A man dressed in all black and wearing a black ski mask was standing between Holly's legs, his hands clasped to the head teller's calves at chest level. His pants and underwear were bunched at his knees and his large, thick cock was pumping back and forth into Holly's juicy pussy.

"Oh yeah! Oh! Oh! Yeah!" Holly cried out with each thrust. "Give it! To me! Oh yeah!"

"Will someone shut her up!" the masked man fucking her said. Two more men in black with masks on were standing on either side of the bank employee atop the bed of cash. Both of the men's pants were down and Holly had their stiff cocks in both of her hands, vigorously jacking them off while they fondled her bouncing breasts. Three other similarly dressed masked men stood in the vault with their pants down, stroking their own hard cocks as they awaited their turn with the teller.

One of the men stepped forward, waddling like a penguin so as not to trip over his pants bunched at his ankles. Holly was screaming out, "Oh yeah! I'm gonna bu--" but her sentence was stifled by a cock being pushed into her mouth. She arched her head back and sucked the robber off while jerking the other two and being fucked by the fourth.

III

"Police! Everybody down!" The loud shouting came from outside the vault followed by a flurry of motion. Agents from the Treasury Department and officers of the Dallas Police Department stormed in and began throwing people to the floor and handcuffing them.

"You're too early! Wait for your cue!" an angry director yelled from outside the vault before he, too, was thrown to the ground and cuffed. Cameramen and other actors in police uniforms were all taken to the floor and systematically frisked and handcuffed.

"Goddammit, I was almost there!" the naked porn star acting as Holly cried out. "You ruined everything!" she said to the police officer who handcuffed her but felt it unnecessary to frisk her.

Taggart looked around with an air of disbelief at the naked woman and half naked guys, one of whom was whining about police brutality and that they broke his dick throwing him to the ground. Taggart had to fight to keep from letting a smile crack his professional demeanor as he followed Michaels to the bundles of plastic wrapped cash.

"Sonofabitch!" Michaels said as he tore open one of the packages and examined a hundred dollar bill. He handed it to Taggart. The image was printed on regular paper and felt nothing like real money that was printed on a cotton blend. Also, these bills were printed a single shade of green and only on one side, the backs were blank.

"I think your bust is a bust," Taggart said as he handed the bill back. There was no way to make a counterfeiting charge stick without a complete bill.

Michaels crumpled the square of paper and tossed it on the floor. He ordered two of his agents to check the rest of the phony money. If they could find even one bill printed with a front and back they might be able to make a case. But probably not.

"Fucking worthless confidential informant," Michaels muttered as he walked away from the porn set. Taggart followed him outside into the hot midday sun. Michaels pulled a tin of Copenhagen from his pocket and offered it to Taggart. Taggart shook his head and Michaels took a dip and stuck it in his lip. He tapped it in place with his tongue and then spit out a few loose particles as he leaned against his car.

"Not quite the quality of your notes, huh?" Michaels said with a laugh.

"You saw them?"

"We've collected a few grand from a couple banks, still tracking them down to which stores they were used at."

"Not quite a super note," Taggart said, "but pretty damn close."

"I heard you caught part of the crew?" Michaels said squinting into the sun.

"I don't think it's a crew. We've got independent operators or possibly rip-off artists, not exactly sure. There are three suspects back in Vegas and at least two more that I'm aware of and trying to track down."

"Well I hope your intel is better than mine. Let's get this shit off," Michaels said as he undid Velcro straps and pulled the ballistic vest off. He popped the car's trunk and they tossed the heavy vests inside. Michaels slammed the trunk closed and said, "How do you feel about a massage?"

"You're not really my type," Taggart said. "But I don't judge if you swing that way."

"Fuck you!" Michaels said with a smile. "Get in the car."

As Michaels drove he said, "When I have a shit day like today's bad bust I go and get a full body massage at this awesome Chinese spa in Fort Worth. It helps get all the toxins and negativity out and clears my head to start fresh."

"Makes sense," Taggart said as he nodded his head. "I don't know that I've ever had a professional massage."

"You're kidding me?"

"I kid you not."

"Well then you're in for a treat. Are you married?"

"Not really," Taggart replied.

Michaels looked at him and smiled. "You're in for a real treat."

The Green Rose Spa was an unassuming business located in a small strip mall nestled between a teeth-whitening business and a consignment shop. Small green letters on a glass door identified the spa, but the windows and door were all covered with closed shades.

A trio of small brass bells jingled as Michaels pulled open the door and stepped inside followed by Taggart. It was comfortably cool inside and the air had a fragrant jasmine smell to it. They were in a small lobby that consisted of a small red, leather couch and an empty desk. A door opened next to the couch and a beautiful, thin Asian in her twenties walked in wearing a silk kimono with red dragons on it. She had long, black hair that touched her curvaceous butt and when she smiled her teeth were so white Taggart figured she must get a discount next door, or maybe trades services.

"Oh Kevin, so good to see you," she beamed and put a little hop in her step as she approached him. She was almost a foot shorter than him and when she reached her arms up to Michaels' neck and hugged him Taggart saw the bottom of her ass cheeks peek out from beneath the kimono.

"Hello my little China doll," Michaels said as he hugged her back and lifted her slightly off the ground. He would later tell Taggart that he called them all that because he could never remember their names.

"This is my good friend, Gary," Michaels said after setting her back on the floor.

"Hello, Gary," she said and gave him a little bow. When she did so her kimono parted slightly to reveal cleavage that needed no bra.

"This is his first time," Michaels told her. "I want you guys to take very good care of him."

Taggart was already feeling a tingling in his groin as he ogled her and tried to imagine what her hands might feel like.

"Oh yes, of course," the beautiful Asian said but then she was grabbing Michaels' hand and pulling him towards the door that she had just entered. "I will send someone good for him. But you come with me."

"She's sending you someone good," Michaels said and gave him a wink before disappearing through the doorway.

Taggart turned around in a small circle, examining the sparse premises and as he came back to where he started he found an Asian lady with a big smile standing in front of him.

"Hello. You come with me," she said and held out her hand to Taggart. He tried not to let his disappointment show to the lady who was old enough to be the first girl's grandmother. She was wearing dark purple tights and a black sweater with wooden buttons. She wasn't ugly and didn't have a bad body for being sixty-something, and he told himself it didn't much matter because he was just getting a massage, right? "Come," she said smiling at him and still holding out her hand. He took it and followed her through the doorway.

V

She led him down a short hallway to a small room that had a massage table, a chair and a tiny shelf with lotion, Kleenex and a CD player upon it. "You get undressed and lie on table, okay?" she told him, her smile never wavering, and then she left the room closing the door behind her.

Taggart piled his clothes onto the chair and then climbed atop the massage table. He'd never been on one before, but he'd seen them in movies and he knew the horseshoe shaped cushion was where his face was to go. He got on his stomach and scooted his body into place and settled his forehead against the toilet seat shaped cushion. He was crushing Gary junior and the boys so he slipped a hand under his hips and readjusted the package between his legs.

There was no towel or sheet to cover up with, so he figured the old lady was used to seeing bare ass and parts sticking out beneath. He thought of her hand and how soft it was as she led him to the room. With her age, he figured, she's got to be quite skilled and experienced and probably gives an amazing massage.

He heard the door open and the soft Asian voice ask, "You ready?"

"Mmm-hm," Taggart said as he stared at the brown carpeted floor beneath the massage table. He heard her move softly across the room and then the click of a button. Gentle flute music filled the room. He heard more soft rustling of movement and then felt the first contact, her soft velvety hand on the back of his right calf. Her hand moved like a warm, gentle breeze up the back of his thigh, over the hump of his ass, then up his back to his shoulder.

Taggart's arms were hanging over the sides of the massage table and he felt the brush of silky fabric against his arm as she slid her hand up his body. His mind was trying to register something but kept getting lost in the sensation of her magical touch that was beginning to make his body tingle all over. She drew her hand across his shoulders and then down his back on the other side of his body. He felt the wispy silkiness of her kimono brush his other arm as her hand slid over his ass and down his thigh and calf and to his foot.

Then it struck him, the old lady wasn't wearing a kimono when he'd seen her. Had she left the room and changed? He wanted to lift his head and look over his shoulder but at the moment he was too mesmerized by the flesh of her hands sliding up his legs. The small, soft yet firm, warm hands slid slowly up each calf at the same time, over the backs of his knees and then up the back of his inner thighs. The edge of her left hand grazed his cock as it moved up his leg to his ass cheeks. The grazing was as soft as a silky cobweb, but it started a fire within him and his cock began to stretch out along the length of his thigh.

The masseuse paid it no mind as her hands and fingers began to knead and massage his butt cheeks. He'd never had anyone do this to him before and it was fucking amazing. He caught himself starting to drool. His cock was stiff with delight, pressed against his thigh and the cushioned table, and every so

78

often he felt the fabric of the silky kimono against the bottom of his feet as the Asian's torso pressed against him and the bottom of her boobs brushed against his heels.

Taggart's stiff cock was aching slightly from its penned position, but he didn't move and let the masseuse continue her magic. He still didn't know if it was the old lady who had changed outfits or a different Asian lady altogether and he didn't really care because whoever it was was doing an amazing job and almost putting Taggart into a trance with her touch. She was standing at the side of the table now, her hands never losing contact with his body as they worked the muscles of his thigh. Every four or five seconds her hand would brush against his thick, throbbing cock and he couldn't tell if it was on purpose or merely accidental as she kneaded his leg. Each time she grazed his hard member he sucked in his breath.

The masseuse's hip bumped ever so gently against Taggart's arm that hung limply from the side of the massage table. A conversation popped into his head, like a cartoon light bulb coming on, of a time he remembered hearing a vice cop talking about entrapment and how they weren't allowed to touch the ladies first because that was signaling to them they wanted something more; the vice cops had to wait until the lady offered first before they could proceed with a proper bust. Luckily Taggart wasn't a vice cop and the only thing he wanted to bust was a nut.

VI

Taggart floated his left hand backwards until he felt the soft flesh of the Asian lady's calf in his palm. He squeezed her gently. He felt her weight shift slightly towards his arm and the fingertips of one of her hands purposely rolled over the tip of his sensitive cock. It caused him to squeeze her a little tighter and this time her fingers brushed over his sensitive, hairy ball sack. Oh, that feels good, he thought.

79

Slowly Taggart slid his hand up the Asian's smooth, slender thigh. He felt the hem of her kimono touch his wrist as he was about halfway up the back of her thigh and his hand kept rising. Her own hand was no longer massaging around his rock hard cock that was pressed tight against his thigh, but was now petting it like a boa constrictor. Her other hand was tickling his balls and fingering the hairs between his asshole and testicles. He couldn't believe how sensitive that area was and how heavenly it felt having her touching him so softly and expertly.

Taggart lifted his hips off the table a few inches to relieve some of the pressure and pain from his pinned penis. The Asian lady's small hand wrapped gently around his cock hanging down, her other hand continuing to stimulate the hairs of his balls and ass. At the same time Taggart's hand had reached her ass beneath the kimono and he squeezed it gently and then slid his hand between her ass cheeks. She was wearing a thong and he rubbed his hand against the soft fabric between her legs.

She stroked his cock between his legs from behind. He was almost up on his knees, his head still pressing against the massage table. His right hand clung to the table bracing himself while his left hand stroked her pussy through the fabric of her thong. Her hips were pressing against him with his hand movements and then she began stroking his cock with both her hands, looking like she was milking a cow. Her delightful hands stroked him up and down while at the same time twisting and squeezing and before he knew it he was spurting his jizz all over the leather massage table, his ass quivering in the air.

The masseuse continued to milk him and then she said, "Don't move." She reached to the small shelf and pulled out a handful of Kleenex, wiping him first and then cleaning off the table. "There you go," she said and left the room with all of the soiled tissues. Taggart relaxed once again upon the massage table with a satisfied sigh.

After about ten minutes he realized the masseuse was probably not coming back, so he got up and put his clothes on.

He replayed it all in his mind and thought how strange it was that he still had no idea what the lady looked like and how that fact made no difference because he felt amazing.

VII

"What do I owe you?" Taggart asked Michaels as they drove back to the office.

"Are you kidding? It's a business expense billed to the taxpayers of America. Did you have a good time?"

"It kind of makes you look forward to a bad day at work."

Michaels laughed and nodded his head. "It's a win-win situation."

"I might have to incorporate your business model back home," Taggart told him.

They reached the office and there were no new developments with the locating of the stores where the counterfeit money from Vegas was spent. "We'll have something by morning," Michaels assured him. "Seeing as you're free tonight, how do you feel about strip clubs?"

Taggart smiled and said, "Now you're talking about my field of expertise. Are your parents' names Angie and Gerald?"

"Huh?" Michaels slowly shook his head.

"I'm starting to think we might be brothers," Taggart said with a chuckle. "Is this an expenditure also on the taxpayers?"

"No, I haven't figured out a way to pull that off yet. We'll need to bring our own money."

Part 6

The Gang's All Here

I

"How much money do we have?" Croak asked as he sat in the passenger's seat of the black Yukon Denali. The truck was parked in the crowded lot that circled Diamond Gentlemen's Club on the east side of Dallas. There were at least three hundred cars in the lot with a constant flow of vehicles coming and going and many people entering and exiting the largest strip club in Texas.

"Real or fake?" BC asked from the driver's seat. His large bulk touched the steering wheel and the top of his bald dome nearly rubbed on the ceiling. He didn't take his eyes off the entrance of the club thirty yards away.

"Real," Croak replied. "Them idiots are already leaving a trail of our funny money."

"I had Paco wire us six G when we were in Flagstaff," BC said.

"Did he get paid off for his sister at the hospital?"

"Yeah. He said she don't like it there no more."

"Not everyone can handle what's required in the nursing field."

Kiki poked her head in between the two front seats and asked, "We going in for some fun or what?"

"Or what," Croak said. "We're sitting here until we know for sure." He looked at BC and asked, "He still here?"

"Hand me my computer," BC said to Kiki. She leaned back and picked up the slim laptop from beside her on the seat.

She was hoping they'd be going inside the crazy busy club. She figured that would be her only chance, to get lost in the crowd, though she didn't doubt for a moment that Croak would shoot her, even in a crowd.

II

"Shoot, look at this crowd," Duncan said as he and Renae walked through the madhouse that was Diamond Gentlemen's Club. Renae looked hotter than any of the more than one hundred and fifty strippers working in the three story establishment. She was wearing a midnight blue dress that reached almost to her ankles that were strapped into three inch heels the color of blood. The dress had a slit in the side that went all the way up to her hip and showed all of her leg when she walked. The top of her dress parted in a V that went all the way to her navel, baring her chest and the fabric barely covering her prominent nipples.

"The crowd seems to be looking at us," Renae said as she walked with her arm looped in Duncan's. Duncan was wearing black slacks and loafers and a cream colored shirt that Renae had picked out for him and which he'd gawked at the five hundred dollar price tag. He'd never paid that much in his life for an entire outfit and Renae had reminded him that he's never had nearly a million dollars in his life either. "I think it makes you look so sexy," she had told him. "Like that one movie star, what's his name, in that speed boat movie?" Duncan had no idea who she was talking about, but if she thought it made him look hot he'd buy two of them.

"It's only you they're looking at," Duncan said as they made their way to one of the six bars in the club. Duncan figured there had to be at least five hundred customers in the place, mostly guys but also couples and even groups of ladies, and Renae was snapping the necks of many of them. They probably figured she was just another worker at the club, but

83

Duncan didn't give a shit what they thought because he knew she'd be leaving with him.

As Renae ordered them drinks Duncan took in the club that reminded him of an open foyer of a shopping mall where you could look up and see all of the upper floors with their glass railings. A huge stage that went from one wall to the center of the club had three strippers on it, two of them on poles and one that was rubbing herself against guys sitting in Sniffer's Row. Two smaller stages were situated in the far corners on the first floor and two more stages with poles and dancers could be seen on the second level on either side of the main stage. Different colored lights rained from every direction and loud hip hop tunes pounded through a hundred speakers.

"Thirty dollars," the bartender said as he placed two tall drinks on the bar. He looked like a pro wrestler in a tight black shirt and though he was smiling he seemed impatient.

"Stacy wasn't kidding when she said everything was bigger in Texas," Renae said as she grabbed her drink and smiled at the bartender.

Duncan pulled out a wad of bills from his pocket and he immediately noticed that they glowed under the black lights like they were radioactive. He quickly shoved them back into his pocket. "We have a problem," Duncan whispered to Renae while looking at the bartender whose smile was faltering.

"Don't worry," Renae said as she opened her Versace clutch, "it'll be my treat tonight." She laid two twenties on the bar, handed Duncan his drink and then pulled him toward a gal she'd been eyeing.

III

"Why do you keep looking at that guy?" Michaels asked Taggart as they stood at a bar on the second floor of Diamond Gentlemen's Club. Michaels was on his second Screwdriver and Taggart was finishing his second vodka and tonic.

"The guy's got a gun," Taggart said. He'd spotted the weapon in the hip holster on the guy while he was bent over talking to a stripper's tits and tucking money into her g-string.

Michaels laughed. "This is Texas, everyone has a gun." He patted his new friend on the shoulder. "Lighten up, man, we're off the clock. Come on, I've got a couple gals I want you to meet."

"You a regular here?"

"Let's just say I've got some CI's here that feed me good intel sometimes. We have a mutually beneficial relationship."

Taggart nodded his head and then felt his phone ringing in his pocket. He pulled it out and looked at the screen.

"Serious?" Michaels asked.

"I don't know the number," Taggart replied. "It could be a lead." He tapped the 'Answer' button. "Hello? Hello?"

Michaels was leaning against the railing watching two women on the main stage below simulating sixty-nine. Both women were completely naked with their mouths inches from each other's pussies, their tits rubbing against each other's abdomens. Ones and fives were fluttering onto the stage.

"That's the second hang up tonight," Taggart said as he approached the railing and put his phone in his pocket.

"I don't care about no phone calls," Michaels said. "I'm here for the pussy. Would you look at that."

IV

"Look at that," Sabrina said with a wide grin. She was a five foot five Hawaiian with long black hair in a French braid. The yellow sunflower dress she had been wearing was laying on the arm of the small brown couch where Duncan and Renae currently sat. Sabrina was now only wearing a white g-string and cheetah print platform heels and she was on her knees between Renae's legs.

Duncan's eyes had been on Sabrina's double D breasts and her perky almond colored nipples the entire time as she

85

undressed and then as she got down on her knees in front of Renae and started sliding her hands up Renae's long legs. Renae's dress easily parted along the slit until it revealed Renae's own slit that was not covered with any panties.

"You're a lucky man," Sabrina said as she looked up at Duncan.

He licked his dry lips and said, "I know." He could barely breathe as he looked at Renae's bare pussy and Sabrina's bare breasts between her legs.

Renae's hand moved between his legs where his hard cock strained against the fabric of his pants. "He's not the only lucky one," Renae said and then smiled at Duncan as she gave him a squeeze. Duncan glanced at the flimsy black curtain that enclosed them in the VIP room on the third floor.

Sabrina looked at Renae's hand rubbing Duncan through his pants and then looked up at his concerned face. "Don't worry," she told him, "no one will bother us in here."

"Really?" Renae asked.

"Really," Sabrina said looking into Renae's eyes. She slid her hands up Renae's body and asked, "May I?"

"Please do," Renae said.

Sabrina slipped Renae's dress off her breasts, setting the twins free. He hands gently cupped Renae's breasts, her thumbs glancing against her excited nipples. "You are sheer perfection," the stripper said as she looked deep into her eyes.

"Thank you," Renae said and then moaned as the stripper's wet mouth encircled one of her nipples. Sabrina pressed her body in between Renae's legs, Sabrina's tits rubbing against the naked pussy and its little patch of heart shaped fur. Renae's left hand was squeezing and stroking Duncan's cock through his pants while her right hand went to the back of Sabrina's head and pulled her tighter into her tit.

Duncan had one arm around Renae's shoulders and his other hand was clawing at the couch cushion. His mouth was bone dry and he could barely speak through haggard breathing. "We better stop. I don't want to have a big wet stain in my shorts."

"We can fix that," Renae said smiling at him. "Excuse me, honey," she said to the stripper as she brought her other hand to Duncan's crotch. Sabrina moved out of the way and watched as Renae unzipped Duncan's slacks and then pulled out his raging hard-on that was glistening with pre-cum. Renae bent over and took Duncan's cock into her mouth. Duncan gasped in pleasure and surprise.

"That's so fucking hot," Sabrina said as she stood watching the two. "Can I finger you?"

"Mm-mm," Renae said as she continued sucking, her mouth sliding smoothly up and down Duncan's shaft.

"Would you like something to suck?" Sabrina asked Duncan as she bent over Renae. She offered him one of her titties while at the same time sliding her hand between Renae's legs. Renae's pussy was wet and Sabrina's fingers slid easily into her, three of them moving back and forth.

Duncan had one hand on Renae's ass and the other cupping one of Sabrina's ass cheeks as he sucked on the stripper's titty, his tongue swirling around her nipple. But all of that was lost in the sensation of his bulging cock and Renae's frantically sucking mouth and head bobbing in his lap. It felt like a fire hose had been turned on as he began spurting his load into Renae's eager mouth and she continued to suck him and swallow him while Sabrina continued fingering Renae.

Duncan eased his head back on the couch as Renae sucked him clean, his ass cheeks quivering uncontrollably. He licked his lips and said, "That feels so good."

V

"We'll make y'all feel so good," the stripper said as she ran her tongue seductively across her bottom lip that was covered with purple lipstick. Taggart wasn't sure if she was Candy and one talking to Michaels was Mandy or the other way around. Not like it made any fucking difference. "Come on, baby, let us take y'all upstairs to VIP."

Taggart was leaning against the railing on the second floor and the stripper was leaning against him with her hands on his chest. She was dark skinned with a thick Texan drawl and Taggart liked the see-through material of her baby blue bra and panties. In her stripper heels she was still a few inches shorter than Taggart and she had her thigh pressed in between his legs.

"I can tell you like me," she said as she looked at him with her big brown eyes. Her pink tongue skimmed across her purple lips again as she rubbed her thigh against the hardness in his pants.

"Whaddya say?" Michaels said from a chair a few feet away. He had a big bootied Latin girl in his lap and her hands were in his half unbuttoned shirt. She was wearing a black skirt and a black tube top that was pulled down to her stomach and displaying her surgically enhanced breasts that looked like they'd just come out of the mold. Michaels had one hand holding her ass in his lap while his other hand held his drink balanced on her thigh.

"Should we take them upstairs?" Taggart asked.

"Now you're talking, baby," Candy or Mandy said to him.

"We should certainly take them somewhere," Michaels said, causing Mandy or Candy in his lap to giggle.

"Holy shit!" Taggart said as he pushed the stripper away from him.

"Hey!" she cried as she wobbled on her high heels.

"It's them," Taggart said.

"Them who?" Michaels said as he pushed the thick girl out of his lap. He could see the intensity on Taggart's face.

"THEM them!" Taggart said as he pushed past the strippers while pulling the gun from his waistband. Michaels was doing the same as they headed for the stairs. "We can't let them get away."

"There they are! Don't let them get away," Croak hollered in the confines of the Yukon. "Come on, go!"

BC was already gunning the motor and pulling out of their parking spot, racing the big SUV towards the front door of the club. Two guys and a gal laughing and heading for the club stepped mindlessly in front of the truck and BC slammed on the brakes. One of the guys held up his hands and the other was helping the gal who had fallen to the ground.

Duncan and Renae were standing in the lot ten yards from the front doors of the club and fifteen yards from the two guys and gal that had almost been hit by the maniac driver in the black truck.

Special Agent Gary Taggart burst from the front door of the club followed by Special Agent Kevin Michaels right on his heels. "Miss Savoy, Stop! Treasury Agent!" Taggart yelled. "You're under arrest!"

Duncan and Renae jerked their heads towards the deep authoritive voice.

"Fantasia!" yelled Kiki from inside the Yukon. Croak had his arm sticking out of the passenger window holding a gun and Kiki hit him in his wounded shoulder as she yelled. Croak fired off a round that went wild, hitting the side of Diamond Gentlemen's Club.

Taggart and Michaels dove for cover and pointed their weapons toward the Yukon. Patrons in the parking lot screamed and ran for cover. Duncan grabbed Renae's hand and pulled her between a row of cars. "Stay down!" he yelled as they crouched and ran.

Croak ignored the pain in his sore shoulder; he'll take care of the Asian cunt momentarily, but first he needed to take care of the fucking thieves. He saw their heads bobbing as they ran between the parked cars and Croak fired off a few rounds. The bullets rattled the cars, piercing metal, shattering windows, setting off car alarms.

"You sonofabitch!" a big Texan in a big hat cried out. "You shot my Caddy!" He pulled out a big gun and fired at the Yukon from the other side of the lot. His bullet missed the SUV and struck a souped up Civic.

"Motherfucker!" a black kid yelled as he jumped out of the Civic with a .380 and fired off towards the Cadillac.

"U.S. Treasury! Drop your weapons!" Agent Michaels yelled.

Croak fired toward the agents who in turn returned fire. Croak and BC crouched down as 9mm rounds slammed into the truck's body and windshield. Kiki pushed open the back door and ran into the mix of cars in the parking lot.

"Kiki!" BC yelled.

"Get us out of here!" Croak said angrily.

BC made one last glance toward the fleeing figure of Kiki. He saw her look over her shoulder at him before she disappeared in the darkness. He slammed the truck into 'Reverse' weaving around vehicles and causing some people to dive out of the way. The parking lot was flooded with people running for their cars, random gunshots, sirens from every direction in the distance.

While BC and Croak bounded over a curb and were racing for the nearest freeway, Duncan and Renae were in the Mustang weaving through side streets in the other direction. Taggart and Michaels wouldn't be able to leave the club for another three hours, but at least they wouldn't be leaving alone.

VII

Mandy was on her hands and knees on the black leather loveseat. She was completely naked, her large breasts swaying with the rocking motion of her body as it moved back and forth. Behind her stood Michaels naked with his hands on her thick hips and his cock plowing in and out of her fat pussy.

Taggart stood on the other side of the loveseat, also naked, his stiff cock fucking Mandy's mouth.

They were in Michael's condo on the forty-third floor of downtown Dallas. Candy came out of one of the bedrooms wearing only a strap-on dildo that was even blacker than she was. "Who do I get to fuck?" she asked.

Michaels smiled at Taggart. "You first."

"Hell no!" Taggart said.

Candy crossed her arms and stuck out her purple painted lower lip in a pout.

"Come here, sugar," Michaels said.

Taggart's eyes grew wide and he stopped pumping his hips into Mandy's face. He couldn't believe Michaels was going to let some chick fuck him and he wasn't so sure he wanted to watch that. He started to go soft.

"I'll go easy on ya," Candy said to Michaels as she patted his ass.

"Homey don't play that," Michaels said. He told Mandy to lie on her side, which she eagerly did. Michaels pushed his cock back into Mandy's pussy and Candy pushed her dildo into Mandy's thick ass. Mandy cried out in pleasure and pain as Michaels and Candy fucked her while at the same time they began kissing and Michaels fondled Candy's tits. All of the action got Taggart hard and he was once again fucking Candy's mouth.

Part 7

Keep On Truckin'

I

"Your mouth is like heaven," Duncan moaned from the driver's seat of his '66 Mustang. Renae was bent over the center console, her knees on the passenger seat and her head in Duncan's lap. Her lips were wrapped tightly around his stiff cock while the fingers of her right hand gingerly cupped and fondled his balls. As she stroked his cock with her mouth his right hand was rubbing her ass that was propped in the air. Renae was wearing a pair of white sweatpants from Victoria's Secret that were as soft as newborn kittens.

"I could live in your mouth," Duncan said as he struggled to keep the car travelling at sixty-five down the interstate. He wished his car had cruise control because he found the car fluctuating five to ten miles per hour in either direction as Renae did her magic.

The sun had come up a couple hours ago and they were somewhere in Mississippi. After the incident at Diamond Gentlemen's Club they had rushed to their hotel, loaded everything in the car and hit the road, driving through the night and into the next day. When Duncan had mentioned he was getting tired Renae offered him a pick-me-up he couldn't refuse.

Now his blood was racing and he wasn't feeling tired but he sure wanted to close his eyes and revel in the sensations of the incredible roadhead he was receiving. It was the first time he'd ever gotten a blowjob while driving and he thought there'd be a lot more cars sold if they all came with this option.

Renae's mouth slipped off the top of his prick and she said, "It gets me so turned on sucking you off." Her mouth slid back over him and engulfed him all the way to his balls.

"Oh really?"

Her mouth popped off his cock and she said, "I love it," and then she sucked him back into her.

"I love what you love," Duncan said.

As soft as her sweats were, he wanted to be touching her even softer flesh and he tried to push her sweats off but they were secured tightly to her waist. Renae slipped her hand beneath her and undid the string and then Duncan was pushing the fabric over the hump of her ass and down to her knees.

"You weren't kidding," Duncan said as he rubbed his hand between her legs and felt how wet she was.

"Hm-mm," Renae replied as her mouth moved up and down Duncan's shaft. He played with her pussy, keeping his eyes on the road, and then slid his slick fingers up and down the crack of her ass. "Mm-hm," came the sound from her bobbing head in his lap.

Duncan's ring finger pressed against her tight asshole and Renae sucked him harder and faster. He didn't know how much longer he could hold on as he cruised down the highway in the left lane. He pushed his finger inside her and her asshole squeezed around him like her lips that were squeezing around his cock.

Renae hummed and moaned as she sucked on Duncan while his finger slid in and out of her asshole. She could feel him about to come and she slid her hand from his balls to his cock and began to vigorously jerk him off as she moved her mouth up and down in motion with her hand.

"Oh god!" Duncan cried and he moved his foot off the gas and pressed it against the floorboard as his cock surged and exploded in Renae's mouth. His hand was slapping against her ass and he realized he had two fingers now fucking her eager asshole.

She continued sucking and squeezing every ounce out of his cock and his hand slowed on her ass. "No, don't stop," she gasped, "I'm almost there." Duncan returned to fingering her faster and harder. His cock was no longer in her mouth but he could feel her breath against him as she panted and moaned.

Duncan glanced at the speedometer and realized he'd dropped down to almost fifty miles an hour. He put his foot back on the gas and then looked over at his hand and fingers going in and out of Renae's little asshole. Beyond the passenger window Duncan realized a big, red Peterbilt eighteen wheeler was keeping pace beside his car. A bubbly trucker in a grey trucker's cap and a bushy black beard was glued to the action in Duncan's car. He gave Duncan a thumbs up.

Duncan kept fingering Renae's ass but twisted his hand slightly to give the trucker a thumbs up of his own. Duncan punched the gas pedal and sped forward as the trucker blew his air horn and Renae began screaming out in ecstasy. Other truckers yanked on their horns as the Mustang shot past with the heart shaped ass bared in the passenger window.

II

"Have you ever been to Mississippi before?" Renae asked as she dipped a french fry into some ketchup on her plate. They were sitting in a small cafe a couple miles off the highway, a place called Mable's. There were three other couples at tables in the small establishment, all of retirement age and all looking with disdain at Renae in her sweats and t-shirt with a big 69 on the front. It was evident she wasn't wearing a bra and Duncan knew she didn't have on any panties. He thought it was hot, fuck everyone else's thoughts or judgments. Their obese waitress had been curt but she was quick to bring them their orders, probably in hopes of getting them out of the cafe as soon as possible.

"I've never been anywhere but Oregon," Duncan said after swallowing a bite of biscuit and gravy. "I think I went to

94

California a couple times with my parents when I was a kid, but I don't really remember it."

"Have you been to Portland?" Renae asked as she picked up her club sandwich.

"Betty and I lived there for three years before moving to Medford."

"I met a girl from there who came to Vegas. She said they have the most strip clubs per capita than anywhere else in the world."

"There are a lot, but I've never been."

Renae set her sandwich down. "You're kidding. Why not?"

Duncan took a sip of coffee. "I don't know. I guess I didn't want to disappoint Betty."

"I'd be disappointed if you didn't go."

"That's why I'm with you and not Betty."

Renae smiled at Duncan and he smiled back. They ate in silence for a few minutes. The waitress slipped the bill onto the table as she walked by, not bothering to ask if they wanted anything else.

"Can I ask you something?" Renae said.

"Anything," Duncan replied as he pushed his plate aside and leaned his elbows on the table.

"Why did you leave Betty?"

Duncan shrugged. "I was bored. Bored of her, bored of us, bored of my life. I'd been an accountant for twenty years, never leaving the state, never doing anything. I didn't even want to get engaged; I only did it because it was what she wanted. I was an accountant because it was what my parents wanted. I got involved in Croak's operation because it was what a friend wanted. I've never done anything in my life because it was I wanted."

"And you've always wanted to go to Miami?"

"Not really. I picked that because it was about the furthest point away from Oregon on the map. Though I did always want to go to Disney World ever since I was a little kid."

"Me too!" Renae exclaimed. A few of the cafe patrons looked over in disgust at her outburst.

"Come on, let's get out of here," Duncan said as he tossed some counterfeit bills atop the check on the table. He took Renae's hand and they left the cafe.

As they drove away, Renae looked in her bag at her feet and then closed it.

"What is it?" Duncan asked.

"Nothing. I keep forgetting that I don't have a phone. It's so strange not having one, like I'm missing a limb or something."

"It's too dangerous. That's how they found me in the first place."

"But we didn't have our phones last night and they still found us."

"I know. I've been trying to figure that out."

"And?"

"I don't know."

"What was Kiki doing in the truck with them guys?"

"I don't know."

"What do you know, Duncan?"

"I know I need to find a hotel because I'm tired."

III

"I'm tired of this shit and my fucking arm is killing me," Croak said as he sat down on the squeaky queen sized bed in the Mississippi motel room. BC sat on the other queen sized bed causing the mattress to almost touch the floor. "What are you sitting down for?" Croak asked.

"I'm tired too," BC said simply.

Croak shook his head. "You've got to ditch the truck and get us another ride."

BC let out a sigh and stood up.

"Don't give me that," Croak said as he leaned back on the pillows. Pain shot through his shoulder and he winced.

"That little bitch got me right in the bullet hole. If I see her again...."

BC was walking toward the motel door, having grabbed the truck keys off a table next to the TV.

"Find me some pain killers," Croak said. "And some pussy. No skinny bitches."

BC nodded his head as he opened the door.

"And a cheeseburger," Croak said as the door swung closed behind BC. "Two of them!"

IV

"There were two different sets of suspects," Agent Michaels said into the phone at his desk, "and you're telling me we don't have a lead on either one? What do you mean what do I want? Review security footage, look for toll booth cameras, check with highway patrol. Do your fucking job!" He slammed the phone down. Michaels looked up to see Agent Taggart with a blank look on his face. "What's wrong with you?"

Taggart's expression didn't change and his voice was monotone. "I just got off the phone with my Vegas chief. One of my contacts, Stacy O'Malley, was found murdered in her home. The last call on her phone was to me."

"You think they got her to call you? Maybe tracking you?" Michaels asked.

"It would explain the unknown calls to my phone last night and how it all went down."

"Maybe we can have tech trace last night's number."

"They can give it a try, but more than likely it was a throwaway phone." Taggart sat down in an empty desk chair and rubbed his temple. "Fuck, we can't even do anything until more of the money shows up, and then we're always two steps behind."

"It's the nature of the beast, man," Michaels said. "You look tense. I know I'm feeling tense. Maybe a massage will help clear our heads and give us a new perspective."

A young Treasury agent that looked like he could still be in high school came into the office. "Agent Taggart? There's an Asian woman here to see you."

Taggart couldn't hide his look of surprise as he looked at Michaels. Michaels smiled and said, "That's pretty damn good when you've got the masseuse coming to you."

Five minutes later Taggart was sitting in an interrogation room across from the beautiful, buxom Asian. She had no make-up on and she'd obviously been crying and looked tired and afraid, but Taggart thought she was still hot as fuck in her short money green dress that showed plenty of leg and even more cleavage. Taggart kept visualizing in his mind the security footage he'd seen of her tits and pussy being waved around the Planet Hollywood Casino.

Kiki told Taggart about being kidnapped and escaping from her captors and how the one called Croak had shot her friend's roommate. She made herself sound like the victim and though Taggart wasn't buying all of her story, he didn't let on and urged her to keep talking.

"That's everything," she told him.

"Do you know where Croak and BC are now?"

"No, I told you. I get away last night. I hide and not see them since."

"So why did you come here?" Taggart asked.

"I think I know where they go next."

"Where?"

"I want to go with you there."

"Not a chance. You're both a witness and a suspect in numerous crimes. I should have you locked up right now."

"I want to help my friend."

"No."

Kiki crossed her arms over her ample breasts and turned her head to look at the wall. "Good luck finding them then."

V

"What do you hope to find in Miami?" Renae asked
Duncan as they sat in a Jacuzzi tub in their motel room. They
had been soaking in the water for about twenty minutes, their
legs rubbing against each other under the water as they talked
facing each other.

"A new life. A new start. I was thinking of maybe buying
a boat and starting a chartering business, maybe do tours to
the Bahamas or something. The world is mine! Ours if you
want to stay with me."

"Do you know anything about boats or the ocean?"

"I can learn."

"What if you don't like it or get bored?"

"Then I'll do something else."

"What if you get bored of me?"

"Not possible," Duncan said and stroked her thigh under
the water.

"You got bored with your fiancé."

"That was different. You're different. The way I feel
about you, how I felt about you when I first met you, I mean,
you're unlike anyone I've ever met before."

"All relationships are like that in the beginning," Renae
said.

"We're in a relationship?" Duncan asked hopefully.

"That's not what I mean," she said as she stood up and
stepped out of the tub.

"Is something wrong?" Duncan asked as he watched her
towel her beautiful, naked body.

"Nothing's wrong," she said, not looking at him. "I'm just
not sure if I'm ready for Miami or not. I've still got a life in Las
Vegas, a roommate, my car."

He didn't know what to say as he watched her walk out
of the bathroom, her lovely ass swaying with each step she
took.

"Are you looking at my ass?" Croak asked.

"Why I wanna look at yo ass?" BC said. "We not even facing your direction."

"Good. Turn the music up. I don't want to hear her slurping on you."

BC reached for the radio on the nightstand and turned the volume up as high as it would go. Kelly Clarkson was pushing her vocal cords to the limit on the Top 40 station. The skinny, white crack whore whose head was between BC's legs was getting her vocal cords tapped by half of the big black cock in her mouth.

Behind them on the other bed was Croak and a heavyset Creole girl with tits that looked like flattened airbags after a car wreck. He didn't care as he had her face down on the mattress and his body was sprawled atop her. He was wearing two condoms as he thrust in and out of her loose pussy from behind. He kept his right hand steadied on her Jell-O ass as he pumped away.

"You're so deep," the large woman beneath him said.

"I told you not to say anything," Croak growled and slapped the woman's face.

"Oh no you didn't!" the woman beneath him screamed.

"Shut up!" Croak yelled and slapped her again.

The woman screamed furiously. She tried to get up and Croak pushed her back down. She tried bucking him off her and Croak rode her like a wild bull, his dreadlocks flying in the air.

"Now we're having fun!" Croak yelled and smacked her flabby ass.

"Stop fucking hitting me!" the woman screamed.

"Stop fucking talking," he said and slapped her again.

"Aaaughhh!" she screamed and tried to roll him off of her. Croak laughed and kept her on the bed as he continued banging her from behind, his hips jerking wildly and his groin clapping against her ass cheeks.

The woman's screams of anger turned to ecstasy as Croak pumped harder and faster into her spasming pussy. He grabbed a fistful of her ass and squeezed until she yelped in pain and then his cock was firing on all cylinders as he shot his load.

Part 8

Atlanta Or Bust

I

Loading the plane took less than fifteen minutes. Taggart and Kiki were sitting in business class, the only seats available side by side at the last minute. It was the government's dime, so Taggart didn't care. Kiki was still wearing the skimpy green dress, though someone in the Dallas office had managed to find her a black sweater that helped cover her shoulders and cleavage. Her high heels and bare legs up past mid-thigh still drew every man's eyes as they boarded the plane.

"Would you two like something to drink before we take off?" a cute blonde stewardess asked them. She was wearing the airline's blue and white uniform that hugged her small breasts and slender hips and she had on flat, sensible shoes. She didn't have much make-up on and her hair was in a short bob cut that framed her face. There was nothing spectacular about her that stood out, but Taggart felt an electric chemistry in her eyes that stirred some childhood memory in him and gave him a tingling in his groin.

Kiki ordered two vodkas. "How'd you know I wanted vodka?" Taggart asked.

"They both for me," she told him.

"Oh, I'll take two, too," he said to the stewardess whose name tag said Chandra.

"I'll be right back," Chandra said and gave Taggart a wink.

"Stare much?" Kiki said as he watched the stewardess move down the aisle.

"Huh? What? I'm a special agent. We're trained to be observant."

"You observed her very good."

Chandra returned with their drinks, handing Kiki hers first and brushing her breasts against Taggart as she leaned across the seat. When she handed Taggart his drinks their hands lingered an extra moment touching each other. "Let me know if you need anything else," Chandra said.

Taggart downed one of the drinks, once again watching Chandra's ass, and Kiki said, "She better get you towel because you probably creamed your shorts already." Taggart choked on his drink. Kiki giggled.

Ten minutes later the plane was preparing to taxi. The stewardess had returned and picked up their glasses and she and Taggart eye fucked for another quickie. Kiki closed the small window next to her seat as the large plane moved onto the tarmac.

"You don't want to watch us take off?" Taggart asked.

"I scared to fly," Kiki told him.

The plane turned onto the runway and Kiki reached for Taggart's hand. He looked at their hands and then at her. "Is okay?" she asked.

He gave her a little smile and nodded. She squeezed his hand tighter.

The plane began to rumble and the engines whined as it picked up speed and shot down the runway. Kiki yanked Taggart's hand into her lap and clasped it with both of her hands as she squeezed her eyes shut. As the plane lifted into the air Kiki squeezed onto his hand harder and pulled him into her. He found his hand pressed between her bare thighs close enough to feel the warmth of her pussy. Taggart found that the plane wasn't the only thing rising.

Fifteen minutes later the plane leveled off and the captain turned off the fasten seatbelts sign. Taggart looked at Kiki and asked if she was doing okay. She didn't reply and he was about to ask again when he realized she was asleep. His hand was still trapped between her silky thighs with her hands holding him.

Chandra had walked by a couple times and smiled, making no obvious notice of Taggart's hand placement. He tilted his seat back and before he knew it he'd fallen asleep. He found himself in a luscious green forest and far off in the distance stood Chandra waving to him and then giggling as she unbuttoned her shirt. Taggart started walking toward her but she had to be far away because she was only about two inches tall.

She was quickly naked, her white body almost glowing in the dark green forest. Taggart called out to her and she laughed and ran away, her tiny ass and small boobs bouncing. He ran after her and when he reached the point where she'd removed her clothes he picked them up to find that they were miniature, only big enough to fit on a two inch tall person.

Chandra called to him and then disappeared deeper into the forest. Taggart ran into the woods and saw her on her hands and knees crawling into a cave in the side of a hill. Taggart's stiff cock was bouncing in front of him as he ran to where he'd seen her lily white ass and bubblegum pink pussy disappear. The hole to the cave was dark and small and he could only fit his finger into it trying to locate Chandra. He knew she was in there because he could feel her kissing his fingertip.

There was an earthquake and the ground began to shake and Taggart awoke to the plane going through turbulence. His right hand felt hot, his finger wet and he looked with wide eyes at his hand under Kiki's dress. Kiki smiled at him.

Shocked, he pulled his hand away. "Sorry," he said. "I was dreaming."

Kiki looked at the bulge in his crotch. "Must be a good dream." He gave her an embarrassed smile. "Do you know about the mile-high club?" she asked him.

"What?"

Kiki undid her seatbelt and scooted past him to the aisle, brushing her hand against his hard cock. She adjusted her dress and told him to meet her in the restroom.

II

BC exited the restroom and walked across the parking lot to the twelve year old white Toyota Camry that he'd purchase for three grand. Croak was tearing open a bag of Flaming Hot Cheetos while in the passenger seat. The whole car shook as the big black man wedged himself behind the steering wheel.

"That bathroom was disgusting," BC said.

"I'm sure you didn't improve matters," Croak said as he chomped on some chips.

BC laughed. "Nobody better go in there for a couple of days."

"Come on, let's get out of here. Are we going to make it before dark?"

BC looked at the small TomTom GPS unit suctioned to the windshield. "I think so. About five hours to go. I can shave off about an hour if I keep it ten miles over the speed limit."

"No," Croak said as he pulled a bottle of orange juice from the center console cup holder. "Keep the cruise control on. We don't need any attention."

BC pulled onto the highway as he chewed on a king sized Snickers. "You think we'll find them there?" he asked Croak who was staring at nothing out the window.

"It was the only address in her book that looked promising. Do you have a better idea?"

BC shook his head. "What if we just dropped it?"

"Too late for that."

"We don't need the money."

"You think this has been about the money?" Croak asked. "If I let Duncan get away with this, then next thing you know Paco is ripping us off and then so is the next punk and the next."

"All this killing means a lot more heat."

"I should have killed that slant-eyed bitch back in that trailer. The only reason I didn't was because I saw you had a thing for her. She's the only witness to any killing. You shouldn't have let her get away from the truck."

BC didn't say anything. He knew better than to argue with Croak.

After a little bit BC asked, "What if they don't show?"

"Then we'll make them show."

"How?"

"From what I could tell, her aunt is the only living relative in her little green book. If she's not living any more, I don't imagine the hooker will miss the funeral."

BC hoped that Duncan and his girl showed up at her aunt's house because he wasn't down for all of the senseless killing.

III

"Killing me softly with his song," Duncan and Renae sang along with the car radio, smiling at each other. Renae was putting on a dramatic performance waving her arms with the music as Duncan bobbed his head in the driver's seat. They were stuck in bumper to bumper traffic in the middle of Atlanta and had only moved a quarter mile in the past ten minutes.

The song ended and a commercial for a car dealership came on. "They don't need to be selling more cars," Duncan said, "they need to be getting rid of some. It's only noon and look at this traffic."

"This is worse than the Vegas strip," Renae said. "This is why I hate Atlanta."

"If you hate it here, why'd we come?"

"My aunt is great. I can't help she lives in a sucky city."

Duncan smiled.

"What?" Renae asked.

"You said sucky."

"You're such a pervert," Renae said and pushed his shoulder.

"Only since I met you."

"Yeah, right. I think you've always been a pervert but were just afraid to express it."

"Maybe. I guess with you I feel like I can say or do anything and it's okay."

"Anything?"

Duncan smiled. "I hope so."

"You perv."

The Mustang moved another ten feet and stopped.

"Are you sure you don't want to just see her now and get it over with?" Duncan asked Renae who was now dancing her bare feet on the dashboard to a John Legend song.

"No, we'll go tomorrow. I've got something else I want to show you first."

Duncan eyed her body thinking about how much he liked when she showed him her things. "I've got all the time in the world," he said.

IV

"Hurry, we don't have all the time in the world," Taggart said.

"You hurry," Kiki told him.

106

"I can barely move."

"Then be quiet and let me do it."

Taggart was sitting on the closed toilet lid in the small airplane bathroom. His jeans and underwear were down around his calves and his knees were pressed together. Kiki's legs were straddling him as she stood with her back to him and her dress bunched around her waist. Taggart's rigid cock was jutting up from his lap and Kiki's bare pussy was riding it up and down as she did squatting motions over it.

Taggart tried to thrust with his hips in motion with her but his positioning was too awkward.

"Relax. I got you," Kiki said.

Taggart pulled her sweater off and then reached around her and freed her enhanced tits from her dress. He squeezed and fondled her large breasts and it took a moment of his fingers roaming all that flesh to find her tiny nipples. They were as hard as little ball bearings.

"Oh, that good," she said.

Taggart had the same thought as she slid up and down his cock, her wet warmth engulfing him and making him feel so good. The plane bounced and tipped slightly and Kiki threw her arms against the bathroom walls to keep from falling.

Taggart squeezed her bouncing breasts harder as he felt the volcano beginning to rumble in his loins. She continued bouncing in his lap, her tight pussy fitting him like a well-oiled glove.

"You tell me when you about to come," Kiki said.

"Oh yeah," Taggart groaned and began shooting his wad inside her.

"Hey!" Kiki said. She tried to get off him but Taggart was hugging her tits tightly and pulling her into him as he jerked his hips against her rump. When he finished spurting into her she stopped bouncing and sat in his lap as he leaned his head on her shoulder.

"You supposed to tell me when you come," Kiki said.

"I said 'oh yeah'."

"I didn't know that what you meant."

"What's the big deal?" Taggart asked.

"I like come."

"Oh, you mean you didn't come?"

"No, I like your come."

"I did."

"You no understand me."

"I'm trying."

The captain's voice came over the intercom informing passengers they were descending into Atlanta and to please fasten their seatbelts.

"We got to go," Taggart told her.

Part 9

Watchers

I

"Should we go?" Duncan asked, keeping his voice low.

"Why?" Renae asked, her voice also barely above a whisper.

Why indeed, Duncan wondered. He had followed Renae as they hiked for ten minutes through the Georgian woods and were now standing at the edge of a clearing. Twenty yards in front of them was a pond about the size of a football field that was more green than blue. Renae had explained to him in the car that it was spring fed and so deep in the middle that you couldn't swim down to the bottom.

The side of the pond they were on had knee high grass that led to the water's edge. The other side of the pond was walled in by a ten foot high rock face topped with trees, some of which had roots hanging down the cliff face. One of the huge trees had a thick, knotted rope swing hanging from one of its branches that stretched out over the pond. A couple birds squawked and played chase from one edge of the pond to the other, disappearing in the trees.

What had stopped Renae on the makeshift trail to the swimming hole were the two people standing knee deep in the water. Well, one of them was standing anyway. It wasn't uncommon to find other people frolicking at the pond and on weekends it could be packed and a line of people waiting for their turn on the rope swing. She had come here a lot as a teenager and once she moved away she always enjoyed making a stop here anytime she'd visit her aunt. It was only about an hour's drive from her place.

But this was the first time she'd ever come upon a couple having sex here. They looked like they were barely out of high school, the guy obviously a jock with his well defined muscles and his short cut wavy brown hair. He was tan except for his ass and hips that were pasty white. The girl squatting in front of him had an average build and was mostly pale skinned except for her tanned arms and face. Said face was currently in front of the jock's groin, her hands on his hips and her golden pony tail bouncing as her mouth slid back and forth on his cock. Renae and Duncan couldn't actually see his cock, either because of their positioning or it wasn't that big. Nonetheless it was obvious what was going on and they were mesmerized by the sight.

"That's kind of hot," Duncan said as he stood behind Renae.

Renae shushed him quietly and then leaned her body into his while she watched the two lovers in the water. Duncan put his arms around Renae's waist, also keeping his attention toward the water.

After another five minutes of sucking the jock's cock, the girl stood up and said something to her man that Renae and Duncan couldn't hear. They saw him smile though and then she was turning around and she bent over. She was facing them but she was looking over her shoulder as her guy positioned himself behind her. Her breasts hung down like two upside down cupcakes with a cherry atop each and they began to sway with her man's thrusting.

Duncan was fully excited and his cock was pressing against Renae's backside as he watched a live sex act for the first time in his life. Renae was wearing a cute blue and white two piece bathing suit they'd picked up on their Dallas shopping spree and Duncan had on a pair of Bermuda shorts with surf boards all over them. The board in his shorts was as hard as could be as he watched the guy fucking the girl from behind.

Duncan's hands had slid their way up Renae's abdomen and were fondling her breast through the fabric of her swim suit. He was kissing on her neck and shoulder, his eyes still watching the couple, and he could hear Renae's breathing becoming heavier. Renae's hands slid to her hips and she pushed her bikini bottoms to mid thigh. She reached behind her and undid the draw strings on Duncan's shorts and pushed down the front of them to free his stiff cock. Renae bent forward while wrapping one of her hands around his member and guiding him into her.

Duncan let out a small moan as he sunk into her warm wetness and pushed deep inside her until his pelvis was snug against her ass. He grabbed the fabric of her bikini top and pulled it aside so he could feel the flesh of her tit, her hard nipple tickling the palm of his hand. Duncan pulled his hips back and then pushed back into Renae's glorious pussy.

Renae reached back and undid her top so the fabric hung from her neck, swinging back and forth as Duncan fucked her from behind. She reached out her right hand and braced it against a nearby tree. Her left hand slid underneath her to her pussy, her fingers feeling Duncan's cock sliding in and out of her as she rubbed her clit for added stimulation.

She looked toward the pond to find the young girl looking at her as they both got fucked by their men. The girl

110

smiled at Renae and then she brought her hands to her tits, her fingers squeezing and pinching her cherry nipples. Duncan's hands were gripping Renae's breasts as his pelvis pounded harder and faster against Renae's ass making small clapping sounds.

Renae bit her lower lip to keep from crying out as her fingers continued their flurry of motion upon her pussy while Duncan's cock jerked back and forth nearing its climax. She felt her's coming like a giant ocean wave that was growing bigger and bigger and then Duncan was shooting his warm jizz into her as the wave came crashing down, flooding her body with warm tingling sensations and causing her legs to wobble and shake. Duncan was pumping and grinding against her ass, his cock quivering inside her as he drained himself, his hands clinging to her tits as if they were life preservers.

Renae held onto the nearby tree for support as she slowly stood and Duncan's semi hard cock slipped out of her. She leaned back into him and he held her tightly, his arms crossed over her breasts and his hands on her sides. They looked at the couple in the water who were now in a different position with the girl facing the jock, her arms around his neck, her legs around his hips and he was holding her ass cheeks in his hands, raising and lowering her as he fucked her standing up. Her tits were rubbing up and down against his chest and she had her head thrown back, her pony tail flopping around as she was fucked for another ten minutes before the boy blew his load.

"That kid has got some stamina," Duncan mumbled in Renae's ear.

"You were eighteen once," she said.

"I was definitely not like that when I was eighteen. I wish."

"I'd say you're doing pretty good for an old guy," Renae said as she reached back and gave his balls a little squeeze.

"Old guy?"

"Come on, let's get in the water," Renae said as she pulled up her bikini bottoms and retied her top. The young couple had put on their swimming suits that were laying at the side of the pond and were now splashing around in the middle as they laughed and played.

Duncan tied the string on his shorts and followed behind Renae saying, "I'm not old. Am I?"

II

"Hi!" Renae said to the couple as if seeing them for the first time. She slipped off her sandals at the water's edge. "How is it?"

"It's really really good," the guy said and his girl blushed. "Jump in."

"Have you tried the swing yet?" Renae asked as she waded into the water.

"No," the girl said, "he's chicken."

"It doesn't look safe," her guy said.

"Duncan will try it out," Renae said and then dove fully into the water.

"I will?" Duncan asked as he made his way into the pond. He thought the water would be colder, but maybe it was just because he was feeling so hot, especially now being close to the couple he'd just watched fucking for the past half hour.

They played at the swimming hole for more than an hour, all of them taking turns on the rope swing, swimming around, and then the girls getting on the guys' shoulders and trying to push each other off. The couple were Brandon and Lacey and were freshmen at the local community college and this was his first time at the pond, though Lacey had been here before. Duncan wondered with how many different guys.

The sun was just about ready to drop behind the trees and Duncan and Renae were talking about heading out when Brandon whispered to the group, "He's back."

"Who's back?" Duncan asked.

112

Lacey looked at Duncan and said, "The guy who was jerking off while he watched you guys watching us." Duncan's face turned red.

"Where?" Renae asked. "I don't see him."

"He ducked behind a tree," Brandon said. "He's there, though, with his dick in his hand."

Renae looked at Lacey and smiled. "Wanna give him something to look at?"

Lacey giggled and nodded her head. The two ladies pulled off their bathing suit tops and threw them to the shore.

"Come here," Renae said to Lacey. When the young girl approached her, Renae put her hands on her new friend's breasts and gave them a squeeze. Lacey returned the gesture and then asked, "Should I, like, suck on them a little?"

"I'd be mad if you didn't," Renae replied.

Lacey giggled, bent forward and sucked on one of Renae's tits and then the other. Renae moaned loudly and dramatically as she fondled Lacey's tits. "Is he looking?" Renae whispered.

"I don't know," Duncan said. "We're too busy watching you two."

"I'm about ready to whip out my own cock," Brandon said half jokingly.

"Dare you," Renae said.

Brandon's eyebrows went up and his shorts came down.

Lacey turned her head and gasped, "Brandon!" as he began to stroke his cock. It wasn't very big, but Renae liked his courage and he obviously knew how to use the thing.

"Don't stop," Brandon told his girlfriend. He waded through the thigh high water and got behind her. Lacey looked up at Renae.

"You heard the man," Renae said, "don't stop."

Lacey smiled and brought her mouth back to one of Renae's tits. She moaned against the soft flesh as Brandon pulled aside her bikini bottoms and slipped his cock into Lacey's excited pussy. He leaned forward as he began to fuck

113

her and put one of his hands over Renae's on Lacey's tit and they fondled her together.

"There he is!" Duncan said.

"Now you're looking for the guy?" Renae said. "Get over here!"

Duncan didn't argue and stepped next to Renae. She undid his shorts and pulled out his semi-hard cock. She wrapped her fingers around him and squeezed. "This isn't exciting you?" she asked.

Duncan looked at Brandon behind his girl pumping his hips while he was bent over her back and playing with her tits with one of his hands. Lacey was still squeezing and playing with Renae's tits while one of Renae's hands played with Brandon's on Lacey's breast and her other hand was stroking Duncan. "Yeah, it's pretty hot," he said.

"Kiss me," Renae said and she let go of his cock and put her hand around the back of his neck, pulling him toward her.

Duncan pressed his body against hers and their mouths came together, their tongues tangling and Duncan's cock shooting to full attention against her belly. One of Duncan's hands cupped her face while his other hand slid down her back and into her bikini to cup her ass. His tongue danced passionately in Renae's mouth and then he felt something else of his in someone else's mouth. He tried to say something as he looked down but Renae sucked on his tongue and kept him in place.

Lacey had taken Duncan's cock in her mouth, sliding it back and forth with the motion of her boyfriend fucking her from behind. She kept one hand on one of Renae's tits and her other hand was cupping Duncan's balls, her fingers tickling his perineum. Duncan closed his eyes and reveled in the glorious sensations.

Renae opened her eyes and peeked past Duncan's head into the forest. She saw the man in his thirties in a dirty white tank top and cutoff jeans at his ankles over a pair of dirty high tops. His hand was vigorously beating his meat, his shoulders hunched over and his hips jerking back and forth as he

114

watched the foursome in the water. The man's hand had started moving so fast it was almost a blur and then he was shooting forth a white stream of liquid love. Renae closed her eyes and concentrated on Duncan's lips and tongue and the hands on her face, tit and ass. She was happy to think someone could have so much fun just watching.

III

Croak hated just sitting and watching. Stakeouts were the worst, hoping and waiting for your quarry to show up. Usually it was a job he paid others to do, when necessary, but now he and BC were given no choice on this journey that had brought them to the suburb outside of Atlanta.

They had arrived on Crestdale Street a little after sunset. The salmon colored home with white trim that belonged to Greta Savoy was a block and a half away and Croak was pretty certain that Duncan and the hooker hadn't made it here to see her aunt yet. Surely they'd stop for more than a ten minute visit, and they couldn't have flown from Dallas because them two were just about as wanted by the authorities as Croak was. So if they'd driven they couldn't be too far ahead of Croak and BC who'd pretty much driven straight through, only stopping at a place called The Great Outdoors to pick up snacks, sodas, binoculars, .40 ammo and a package of travel toilets.

The sun was rising as Croak pulled one of the travel toilets out of the four pack, his second since they'd parked. The package wasn't much more than a plastic bag and a pee hole and inside was some sort of chemical that hardened to a gel when liquid hit it. Croak could have just as easily pissed into empty soda bottles; he didn't care much for all of the fancy-shmancy new age technology. He unzipped his pants, pulled out his willy, stuck it in the bag he positioned between his legs and let loose with a stream of relief.

BC awoke in the passenger seat and looked at Croak.

115

"Don't watch," Croak said. "You know I get stage fright."

BC turned his head and looked out the window while Croak finished and zipped up. "I need one of those," BC told him. Croak sealed and tossed his used bag on the backseat floorboard and then fished one out of the pack for BC. Croak turned his head away while BC untied the waistband of his designer sweat pants.

"How do you do this shit?" BC asked as he fumbled with the plastic package.

"Stick the bag between your legs and put your dick in the hole."

"There ain't no room for me to spread my legs in this small car."

Croak kept his eyesight the other direction as he said, "Then just pull your dick up and do it. Everyone knows the thing's long enough."

"Yeah, well then you also know it's too big to fit into this little bag's piss hole."

"I didn't check to see if they made any for Sasquatch."

"You think that shit's funny, but I seen him."

"I know, I know."

"Twice."

"I know. You gonna piss or not? My neck's starting to hurt."

"I'll hold it," BC said. "How much longer?"

"I don't know. Let me call them and ask approximately what time they'll be arriving so we can get our shit back and kill them."

"You been up all night?"

"Yeah. That's kinda what you do on stakeouts."

"Croak, you remember when a long time ago you told me to tell you when you were being a dick? Well, you're being it."

Croak looked seriously at his partner. "What are you talking about? I'm always a dick."

"You're always a dick in general. But now you're being a dick specifically to me. I'm starting not to like it."

116

Croak was about to say something but he was pretty sure it would sound dick-ish so he bit his tongue. He looked toward the salmon colored house and watched the shadows on the yard disappear as the sun rose higher in the sky.

He and BC had been partners for nearly eight years but he felt like the big guy was getting soft. He wasn't sure if it had something to do with little miss slant eyes that they'd picked up and lost or if BC was simply losing his nerve for the game.

They had met in county jail where Croak was awaiting trial for armed robbery of multiple marijuana farms. One of the guys he'd allegedly robbed had a few homies also in lock up and had sent them to do a number on Croak. While Croak was getting his ass handed to him by three Mexicans, BC had put a stop to it, sending two of the attackers to the hospital when he bashed their heads together. Croak had beat his robbery charges and had also paid big bucks for his attorney to represent BC who was being railroaded for having sex with two deputy sheriff's wives at the same time. Their husbands had forced them to cry rape and because BC was a big, scary black guy he would have been toast without the high paid attorney who got him off. BC felt he owed Croak his life and they'd been inseparable ever since.

"You get any sleep?" BC asked.

"No."

"Aren't you tired?"

"Do I look tired?"

IV

"You look tired," Taggart said.

"I am tired," Kiki replied.

"Why are you tired, I did all the work last night." Kiki smiled from the passenger seat of the charcoal grey Chrysler 200. The rental car was parked at the cross streets of Crestdale and Lois; from the driver's seat he could see the front of Greta Savoy's home half a block away. They'd been parked there since sunrise less than an hour ago and Kiki had been struggling to keep her eyes open.

"I not a morning person; I tell you that."

"I told you, you could have stayed at the hotel."

Kiki shook her head. "I come."

Taggart smiled wide.

"What funny?" Kiki asked.

"You come."

She looked confused and then smiled. "Oh, because I like come?"

Taggart had never seen anything like it, the way this girl was about come. He had fucked the shit out of her in the hotel room last night but this time he'd done as she'd asked and spurted his come all over her belly, tits and face and she'd spread it around her body like it was some new age cream. A couple hours later he found her between his legs licking and sucking on his hard cock and as he neared completion and got ready to blow he felt her finger drive into his asshole and touch something inside him that was like a release valve. Taggart howled as his prick exploded like a broken fire hydrant and Kiki lapped at it like a puppy trying to get water from a hose.

"You're crazy about come," Taggart said.

"Someday I gonna do bukkake party."

"Boo what?"

"It's party with lots of men and I in the middle and I jerk them or suck them until they all come on me."

"At the same time?"

Kiki nodded and smiled. "Sounds fun, right?"

"I don't know. Whatever rocks your boat I guess."

"How long we gonna be here?"

"As long as it takes. You can lie down if you want. I'll let you know if anything happens, okay?"

"Promise?"

"Promise."

Kiki lain with her head resting on Taggart's thigh. After a little while she shifted her body around so that her face was pointing toward Taggart's crotch. Something in him wasn't

118

sleepy at all and began to rise up and Kiki was soon unzipping him and letting the one-eyed snake out which she caressed with her lips and tongue. Taggart leaned his head back against the seat and kept his eye on the house while Kiki's head bobbed up and down.

"Put your seat back," Kiki told him.

"No, I've got to watch the house."

"I watch it. Put your seat back so I can ride you."

There was no way he could logically refuse that request so Taggart reclined the seat down until it was touching the back seats. Kiki's green dress was already pulled up over her hips and she climbed on top of him, her knees straddling him and her ass facing him. Taggart placed his hands on her ass and spread her ass cheeks as he watched his cock sliding in and out of her pink pussy.

V

"The pink house?" Duncan asked.

"It's salmon colored," Renae said. "Pull right into the driveway. Aunt Greta doesn't drive."

"Who doesn't drive in this day and age?"

"It's not that she doesn't, she can't. Aunt Greta likes her drink and had a few too many DWI's. It was either give up her license or go to jail. She doesn't like the taste of hootch in jail."

They got out of the car and Renae took Duncan's hand.

"There they are!" BC said as he saw the maroon Mustang turn into the driveway of the house.

Croak and BC got out of their car at the same time Duncan and Renae did and moved quickly along the row of parked cars in the street. When they reached the corner, they crossed the street to the corner kitty corner from the one they were at.

Kiki's wet pussy slid happily up and down Taggart's pole and she liked his hands spreading her ass cheeks apart. The windows were beginning to fog up, but not enough where she couldn't notice Croak and BC at the far end of the block crossing the street.

"Oh shit!" Kiki screamed.

"Are you coming?" Taggart asked. It took him a moment to realize she wasn't coming but rather was going as she shoved open the driver's door and fell off his dick and landed in the street on her hands and knees. She was quickly to her bare feet and running towards the salmon colored house.

"Would you looky here," the tall, thin gray haired lady holding a drink said as she opened the door to see her niece and a handsome looking man. She stepped out onto the stoop and Renae gave her a big hug.

"Aunt Greta!" Renae said as she hugged the woman who hugged her back with one arm and keeping her drink outstretched in her other. "I've missed you."

"I've been right here," her aunt replied.

Renae let her go and asked, "Is that a Harvey Wallbanger?"

"It ain't green tea."

Renae smiled at Duncan and said, "She loves her Wallbangers. Auntie, this is Duncan."

"Hi, Duncan," she said as she shook his extended hand. Her gaze went over his shoulder. "Isn't that the darndest thing you ever saw?"

Duncan looked over his shoulder and Renae did the same. Kiki was running barefoot down the middle of the street. The money green dress she was wearing kept riding up her hips exposing her bare, glistening pussy and one of her bouncing breasts had slipped free exposing her tiny dark nipple.

"Look out! They're coming!" Kiki screamed as she pointed further down the street.

All three people on the porch turned to look the other direction and saw the skinny dreadlocked Croak and the super sized BC walking quickly their way.

"Where the hell did she come from?" Croak said as he pulled out his gun from beneath his poncho.

BC felt a flutter of butterflies in his stomach, excited at seeing Kiki, and he ran towards her. Croak was still walking briskly toward Greta Savoy's house and pointed his gun at the three people frozen on the front stoop of the home.

A charcoal grey car skidded around the corner half a block behind Kiki. Croak saw Agent Taggart behind the wheel and he fired his gun at the car.

"Kiki, get down!" BC yelled and she took heed and ran toward the sidewalk.

On the front step of Greta's house Duncan grabbed Renae's hand and yanked her toward the Mustang. "Auntie! Lock the door and call the police," she yelled as she was pulled to the car.

The Chrysler 200 barreling down the street swerved toward BC and he jumped onto the hood of a nearby car, denting it as if were struck by a boulder. Croak fired off three more rounds at the oncoming car, one of which pierced the windshield and struck Taggart in the right shoulder. The Chrysler slammed into two parked cars in front of Greta's house and came to a stop, smoke rising up from the hood.

As Duncan pulled Renae into the Mustang, she was looking out at Croak with the gun in his hand firing at the gray car. As soon as the car crashed he redirected his gun toward Kiki.

Renae yelled, "Kiki! No!"

Croak fired.

BC had rolled off the hood of the car and his large bulk rose up in front of Kiki. Croak's bullet struck BC between the shoulder blades.

"No!" Kiki screamed as BC fell hard to his knees. He was looking at her with unseeing eyes as he crashed to the sidewalk face first like a felled tree. Kiki saw Croak standing behind him with his gun still pointed at her.

Duncan's foot floored the gas pedal and the Mustang rocketed backwards slamming into Croak, causing him to drop his gun as he clung for dear life to the trunk of the car to keep from falling beneath the car and being run over. The car shot across the street and hit a three foot high chain link fence circling someone's yard, stopping the Mustang's momentum.

Duncan slammed the car into 'Drive' and the tires smoked and squealed as it peeled away from the fence and left Croak behind, battered and bruised.

Renae yelled at Duncan that they had to get Kiki and he slammed on the brakes next to the sidewalk and Renae leaped out of the car and pulled a shocked Kiki back into the Mustang. In a squeal of tires they raced down the street and around a corner.

Croak ignored the nosey neighbors coming out of their homes as he quickly hobbled back to the Camry a block and a half away.

Inside the Chrysler, Taggart lay bleeding and he was pretty sure his right lung had collapsed. Painfully he reached down and tucked his cock into his pants and then spoke weakly into his radio: "Officer shot. I need help."

Part 10

Getting Help

I

"Of course we'll help you," Renae told Kiki. "Won't we, Duncan?"

"Only if she promises not to hit me over the head again," he replied.

"Duncan!" Renae said and gave him a dirty look.

The three of them were sitting in a halfway decent motel room an hour south of Atlanta. They had driven in almost complete silence save for some crying and sniffling from Kiki as Renae hugged and comforted her. Renae had fixed Kiki's dress to cover her but in hugging and at times rocking her like a small child the top of the dress had slipped and Duncan couldn't help looking at her nipple every time he glanced at the two women in the seat beside him.

Unlike the first motel room the three of them had been in together, this one had two queen sized beds and no headboards that anyone could be handcuffed or tied to. Renae and Kiki were sitting on one of the beds as he sat in a chair next to a table in front of a large plate glass window that had the orange curtain pulled tight over it.

"I just want to go back home," Kiki said. "I'm scared."

"That's why you should stay with us," Renae told her as she looked at Duncan. He tried to keep any emotions from showing on his face. Renae continued, "We're going to Disney World. We're gonna have a lot of fun."

Duncan remembered the fun he had less than a week ago with Renae and Kiki. He had to admit he had the time of his life, at least until Kiki had almost killed him. His head was still tender from where she'd smacked him with a billy club. He wasn't sure if he really wanted her anywhere around and yet he couldn't keep his eyes from drifting, from her tits bulging in her green dress down to the hemline that was barely covering her pussy. He'd already seen it once in the motel room when she'd scooted forward on the bed and the fabric rode up her legs.

Kiki shook her head. "No, I need to get back." She wiped her eyes and nose with a Kleenex that Renae had given her. A dozen crumpled tissues littered the nightstand next to the blue Kleenex box. "Do you think there a way to find out if Taggart okay?"

"Who's Taggart?" Renae asked.

Kiki looked at her girlfriend and her eyes grew wide as if she'd just seen a ghost. "Oh god!" Kiki sobbed and began crying uncontrollably. Renae hugged her and told her it was alright, everything was going to be okay. She looked toward Duncan and shrugged her shoulders.

Kiki got herself somewhat under control and wiped her face with more tissues Renae handed her. She blew her nose and then looked at Renae with her red eyes full of hurt and compassion. "You don't know, do you?"

"Know what?" Renae asked and it suddenly felt like her stomach had fallen through a trap door. She knew the look on Kiki's face wasn't good and she knew she didn't want to hear whatever she was going to tell her.

"They killed Stacy," Kiki said.

"What?" Renae said as she quickly stood up. "No. They - no." She shook her head. "No."

"I'm sorry," Kiki said.

"Nooo!" Renae cried out and then her legs went weak.

Duncan jumped out of his chair and grabbed her before she fell. Renae clung to his chest and soaked his shirt with her tears. Kiki scooted off the bed and Duncan couldn't help noticing her dress riding up and baring her pussy. He looked to the ugly red and brown carpet because he figured this was no time to get a boner. Renae was right, he was a perv. Kiki pulled some tissues from the box on the nightstand and handed them to Renae.

Duncan sat her on the bed next to Kiki and he stayed beside her holding her up. Kiki hugged her from the other side, her hands brushing against Duncan's arms and one of her breasts pressing against his hand. After a few minutes Renae got hold of herself enough to ask, "Why would anyone have reason to kill Stacy?"

Kiki shook her head. "Because Croak fucking crazy."

II

"Croak, that's fucking crazy."

"Just do it!" Croak said into the phone. "Find out if she's heard from him or if he's got friends or family somewhere down here. There's got to be some reason he's travelled this far, and not just because of the hooker he's with."

Paco ran his fingers through his black hair and asked, "What hooker?"

"That doesn't matter, just find me some idea where he might be."

Paco switched the phone to his other ear. "Why would she tell me anything? The lady doesn't even know me."

"Fucking figure it out!" Croak yelled and Paco jerked the phone away from his ear. Croak was still yelling, "Beat it out of her if you have to!"

Two hours later Duncan's ex-fiancé was screaming for dear life as Paco pounded her. He put his hand over her mouth and she bit it. Paco yelped and yanked his hand away and at the same time stopped pounding Betty.

"Don't stop," Betty begged.

Paco smiled and thrust his hips forward and resumed pounding her. Betty screamed in delight as she met the Mexican's every thrust with thrusting of her own.

Paco didn't take her for a screamer when he'd first shown up at her house. The place was an unassuming small home on a quiet street with a Dodge minivan in the driveway. He hoped that didn't mean there'd be kids because that could be a problem. A sick fuck like Croak would use the kids as leverage, threaten to hurt them or something, but Paco could never do that; he didn't even like to smoke or drink in front of kids. He didn't want to set a bad example because he figured the world was already full of enough messed up people.

Luckily it was only Betty in the house and when she answered the door she was almost as unassuming as everything else. She was wearing an unflattering yellow dress that looked like it could have been made from old house curtains which stopped six inches above her scuffed brown boots. Her dark hair was in some sort of pony tail that was bobby-pinned to the back of her head. She wore no makeup on her thick lips or puffy cheeks, and though her hazel eyes were pretty, they were covered by thick white framed glasses that were much too big for her face.

"Um, hi," she said when she opened the door. The Mexican standing in front of her was an inch or two taller than her and that was only because he was wearing cowboy boots. He was built like a solid tree trunk that had been stuffed into a pair of Wranglers and a brown flannel shirt that was buttoned all the way to the collar. Betty figured him to be mid-twenties and it crossed her mind that she could have been his babysitter when she was in her teens. She brushed that silly thought away and asked, "Can I, um, help you?"

"My name's Paco," he said with a winning smile.

Betty instinctively gave a half smile back. She smelled his cologne for the first time and it made her lean unconsciously forward. His dark brown eyes never left her's. "Do I..." she shook her head. "Have we met?" She tried to place his face, wondering if he was a student at the community college where she worked, but he wasn't familiar.

"Croak sent me," Paco said.

Betty stepped back, almost tripping over her feet. Her pale face turned even whiter, as if it had just been covered in talcum powder, and her eyes filled up with tears. She started hyperventilating.

"Hey, you alright?" Paco asked. Betty bent over and placed her hands on her knees as her chest heaved for air. Paco stepped into the house and put his arm around her back, his hand accidentally resting against the side of her breast. "Relax, it's okay," he told her. "Come on, let's sit you down." He pushed the door shut with his boot and then helped her to a black fabric couch with shiny, worn cushions.

"I-I-I-I-" she said gasping for air.

"Shh," he told her. "Bend over, put your head between your knees. There you go. Now just calm down." Paco began rubbing her back in large circles, his hand bumping over the ridges of her bra. "That's better," he told her as her breathing slowly returned to normal.

She kept her body bent across her thighs and she stared at the fringes of the zebra striped rug where it met the hardwood floor beneath her feet. When she thought she had it together, she said, "I haven't tried to contact Duncan, I promise I haven't." She then started bawling.

"Betty, it's okay. I believe you. I'm not here to hurt you."

"Y-y-you're not?"

"No, I just wanted to talk to you."

"But I don't know anything. Really. Oh god, I feel like I'm going to faint."

"Here, lie down," Paco said as he stood up and then gently lay Betty on her back. He lifted her legs and softly straightened them the length of the couch. He put his hand on her forehead and said, "You're burning up. I'll be right back."

Paco rushed out of the room and returned with a cup of water and a cool damp towel. He began patting her forehead and cheeks which had a light sheen of sweat on them. He pulled her glasses off and set them on the coffee table next to the water.

"Can I have a drink of that?" she asked.

127

"Yes, it's for you." Paco stood beside her and brought the cup to her lips. She tilted her head up and drank greedily and water ran down her chin and onto her chest. "Oh, sorry," he said and with the towel in his other hand he dabbed at the spilled water on her neck and chest.

"Ooh, that feels good," Betty said as the towel pressed against her chest. Her dress had six buttons down the front of it and she undid the top two and pulled the fabric apart. It still covered her breasts fully but Paco could see the strap of her light pink bra and it caused a hint of excitement in him.

Betty's hand touched his with the towel in it and pulled it to her chest and the little skin she bared. "I don't know why I'm so hot," she said. "I'm burning up."

"Yes, you are," Paco said, finding himself also feeling hotter by the second. "Do you want more water?"

She nodded her head and lifted it again as Paco brought the cup to her lips. Her eyes watched Paco and he watched more water dribble down her chin and onto her chest. He dabbed at the spill as he pulled the cup away.

"Wait, pour it on me," Betty said.

"What?"

"The water."

"You want me to pour it on you? Your body?"

She nodded. "Hurry."

The cup was less than half full and he tipped it over Betty's chest and on her dress between her breasts.

"Is that it?" she asked.

"You want more water?"

"Yes."

Paco dropped the towel on the floor and ran into the kitchen with the cup. He filled it with cold water and then grabbed an even larger mug and filled it too. When he returned to the living room Betty was still lying on the couch and was finishing unbuttoning the last button on her dress. The fabric split open at her navel and spread wider in a V up her torso, the dress still covering most of each breast.

Betty didn't know what was wrong with her and wondered if this was one of those hot flashes that her mother had told her about. But she'd only just turned forty, so surely she wasn't old enough for that, was she? She was even more scared that it could be signs of a heart attack or stroke or something. All she knew was that she was burning up and she needed to cool down. If she didn't think she'd faint she'd have tried to get to the bathroom to turn on the cold water in the shower.

"I have more water," Paco said standing beside her.

"Do it," she told him.

He poured the mug of water up and down her body, making her gasp, watching it splash between her breasts, the edges and front of the pink bra now exposed over her milky white skin. Water pooled in her belly button and slid down her sides into her dress. Paco found it arousing and his Wranglers became a little snugger.

"Oh yes," she said. "Will you take off my boots please?"

He set the empty mug and full cup of water on the coffee table and then began to untie and remove her boots, dropping them to the floor along with her pink socks. As he turned back around to face Betty, she was reaching for the cup on the coffee table but struck the bulge in the front of his pants.

"Oh god, I'm sorry," she said.

Paco's face turned red. "No, don't be, it's me."

She looked up at him. "It is you what?"

He looked into her eyes. "I'm sorry, you're just so...wet. And beautiful."

Betty blushed. "You think I'm...beautiful?"

"Very," Paco said as he licked his lips and looked her body up and down. He looked back down into her hazel eyes and nodded his head. "Very."

She looked at the bulge in his jeans and asked, "Aren't you hot, too.?"

He licked his lips again and nodded his head.

She reached out her hands and began to undo his belt as Paco's fingers fumbled with the buttons on his shirt. His chest

129

was bare as Betty pulled his pants down to his knees. He tried to kick off his boots and then tripped and fell to the floor on his ass.

Betty gasped and asked if he was alright.

"No, you're making me crazy," he told her with a smile.

That was the hottest thing she'd heard in a long, long time and she sat up and wiggled out of her dress as Paco got his boots and pants off. He stood up, his red and gold boxers poking out in front of him, and he looked at Betty wearing only her pink bra and white cotton panties with flower prints. Their eyes locked onto each other.

"You need more water?" Paco asked.

Betty shook her head. "Show me I'm beautiful," she whispered.

Paco stepped out of his boxers, his cock springing out of a black bush of pubic hair. He wrapped his fingers around the waistband of Betty's panties and pulled them tenderly down the length of her legs and dropped them atop her socks and boots.

Betty spread her legs as he got onto the couch between them, his eyes transfixed on the brown patch of hair that covered her pussy. Then his cock was splitting her open and sinking into her and they both sucked in their breath. Betty cried out, "Oh yes!"

"Oh yes," Paco repeated as he began moving in and out of her like a well-oiled piston. Betty began to get louder and louder as Paco fucked her faster and harder. Her wet body was going wild beneath him as she thrust her hips into his oncoming thrusts and she screamed out as multiple orgasms exploded like the Fourth of July in her crotch and belly. Paco kept pounding and then his dick was shooting off rockets of its own inside the screaming woman.

Paco laid atop her for some time, their heartbeats practically thumping against each other's chests. Betty's fingertips were making long stroking patterns up and down Paco's strong back.

"Thank you for making me beautiful," she whispered in his ear.

"That's not something I made you. That's something you are."

She squeezed him in a hug.

"I guess it's hard to feel that way after my fiancé ran away."

"Duncan is a fool," Paco said. "He's a fool for giving up on you and even more of a fool for stealing from Croak."

"I really don't know where he is."

"I believe you. But he must have family or friends."

"They said he was in Las Vegas."

"Not any more. He's halfway across the country."

"He is?"

"Before he left did he talk about any places he wanted to go to or friends he might want to visit?"

"His only friends are here in Oregon."

Paco propped himself up on one arm and touched her face with his other hand and then traced a finger along the cup of her bra she still wore. "Think, Betty, was he acting strange or saying anything out of the ordinary his last week or so?"

She shook her head slowly as her hands ran over Paco's ass. "No. Well, he was humming and singing some stupid song."

"What song?"

"I'm going to Disney Land."

"Disney Land or Disney World?"

"What's the difference?"

"About three thousand miles."

"I don't know if that helps," Betty said.

"Me neither. But I should call Croak."

"After you call him, will you stay with me tonight? I don't want to be alone."

III

Kiki didn't want to be alone and she was curled up in a ball under the covers with Renae spooning her from behind. Duncan finished taking a shower and after drying off he got in bed and snuggled up behind Renae. He could feel that both of the ladies were naked and nature quickly took over.

"Really, Duncan?" Renae said.

"I can't help it," he laughed.

Renae wasn't laughing. "I can't do this right now. Will you sleep in the other bed?"

"Seriously?"

"It's been a traumatic day. Can you just give us a little space?"

Duncan got out of bed and got dressed. As he walked toward the motel door Renae asked, "Where are you going?"

"Giving you space," he said and pulled the door shut as he walked out. He started up the Mustang and pulled out of the lot.

They were in a city about an hour south of Atlanta, not far from where he and Renae had turned off to go to the swimming hole yesterday. That seemed like a lifetime ago. Duncan couldn't figure out how Croak or the Treasury Agent could have possibly known to find them in Atlanta. Neither he nor Renae had a cell phone, so they weren't being tracked that way. He wondered if maybe there was a tracking device on his car, which would also explain the Dallas encounter.

They should never have gone to Renae's aunt's house. If they were going to remain free they needed to cut ties to anyone that knew them at all. Renae had called her aunt after they'd reached the motel, telling her to get some place safe.

"The street is swarming with police," Greta had said. "There's no place safer than my house right now. By the way, there's some government agents here that want to ask you some questions."

"I can't," Renae told her. "I'm okay. I'll be in touch," she said and quickly hung up the phone.

Now Duncan found himself aimlessly driving through the small city and he realized he was on a street lined with car lots. He loved his Mustang, had it for almost a decade, but he knew he had to get rid of it if he was going to remain free. His plan was to sell it in Miami, but why did he have to wait until then? Especially having Kiki with him tonight, he could park his new vehicle away from their motel room so if Kiki got froggy and tried to rob him again, she wouldn't even know which vehicle was his. He thought it was a brilliant plan.

"How can I help you?" the slick, gray haired salesman asked Duncan after he got out of his car.

"Looking to trade in my classic car," Duncan told him.

"That a '67?"

"'66."

"What you looking for?"

"I'm not sure."

The salesman told him to look around while he had his mechanic check out the Mustang. Duncan found a beige GMC Terrain that looked clean and spacious. He waved the salesman over and asked, "How much?"

IV

"How much?" Croak asked as he sat in the white Camry.

A heavyset white girl in golden pigtails was standing on the curb. She had on tight blue booty shorts that must have taken a magical feat to pull over her thick thighs. She wore a matching blue halter top that held her tits like a couple of baseballs in a sock over her flabby stomach. She bent down and poked her head near the open passenger window, but not close enough to be grabbed. She'd been working the streets too long for that to happen a third time.

"What are you looking for, sugar?" The make-up on her face was too much for Croak's liking, but her body was ideal and that's all he really wanted right now.

He kept his eyes on her tits and said, "All night."

"You gotta hotel room?" she asked as she chewed on a piece of gum.

"No, you have to get it. I'll pay for it."

"I don't know," she said, not liking the vibe she was feeling from the guy. Then she saw the wad of money that he pulled out of his pocket. Business had been slow and her ankles were hurting from standing in her stupid high heels; it would be nice to lie down for a little while and not have to come back out tonight. "A hundred for the room and four hundred for the night," she told him and held her breath. She expected him to laugh in her face or at least bicker over the price and she was prepared to do it for half that.

Croak held up five hundred dollar bills.

"My name's Heidi," she told him as she got into the car. "What's yours?"

"Croak," he said as he pulled away from the curb. "Which hotel?"

"I've got something better," she told him and directed him to her small apartment a few blocks away. She didn't usually bring tricks here but it would mean an extra hundred bucks in her pocket and would be more comfortable than some sleazy hotel.

Croak followed her into the small one bedroom apartment that had magazines and clothes scattered around the living room. The place smelled like pumpkin. On a kitchen counter a lone blue Beta fish swam back and forth in a fishbowl.

"Do you mind if I take these off?" Heidi said as she leaned against the counter and began to unfasten her heels. "I think there might be a beer or something in the fridge."

"Do you have a bathtub?"

"You want to take a bath?" she asked incredulously as she removed her second shoe. "Well yeah, sure. It's in here."

He followed her to the small bathroom. "I don't know it's big enough for two, but there it is." She was about six inches shorter than Croak without her heels and she looked up at him. "Want me to run the water?"

134

Croak nodded. "And then help me with this."

"I didn't even know they still made ponchos," she said after the water was running and she was helping him remove his clothes.

"Ever been to Mexico?"

"Huh-uh," she replied cluelessly.

"Go get me that beer," he told her as he eased into the hot water.

Twenty minutes later she was kneeling beside the tub as she gently slid a bar of soap over Croak's body. His chest was purple and blue from being rammed by the Mustang and the skin around his bandaged bullet wound in his shoulder was an angry red.

"I'm pretty broken," he said to her as he finished the bottle of Heineken and set it on the floor.

Heidi's hand was soaping up his hard cock under the water. "Not all broken," she said and gave him a smile.

Croak leaned his head back as her soft hand squeezed and stroked his shaft. He stretched out his arm and cupped one of her breasts in his hand, squeezing it through the fabric of her tube top.

"Ow! Be gentle," Heidi said as she continued stroking his cock, creating small waves in the tub.

Croak opened his eyes and glared at her. He pulled her blue tube top down and gripped her tit like it was a doorknob, squeezing and twisting it.

"Ow!" she screamed and then wrapped her hand around Croak's balls and squeezed until he yelled out in pain. He loosened his grip and she did the same. "See, that shit hurts," she said.

"You fucking hurt me," he said.

"You hurt me first. I don't go for that shit."

"I want you to kiss it and make it better."

"You first," she told him.

"Come here."

Heidi leaned forward so her bruised tit was in front of his face. She kept her hand on his stiff cock, ready to grab hold of his balls if he tried anything.

Croak leaned forward and placed a ring of gentle kisses around her areola and then slipped her hardened rosy nipple between his lips and sucked and stroked it with his tongue. Heidi moaned pleasantly.

"Your turn," he told her. He let his midsection float near the top of the water, his rigid cock rising like a submarine periscope.

Heidi pressed his cock against his abdomen and bent over the edge of the tub. She tickled his scrotum hairs as she rained kisses upon his ball sack.

"French kiss," Croak said.

She smiled at him and sucked his balls into her mouth. Croak smiled back as he put his hand to the back of her head and then dropped his hips to the tub bottom and pushed her head under the water. Heidi spit his balls out of her mouth and splashed her hands in the water as she tried to lift her head out of the tub. Croak laughed at her struggling and finally jerked her head out of the water.

Her make-up was smeared and one of her pig tails had come undone and she looked at Croak with terror and rage. She spit water out of her mouth and screamed at him. "You fucking--"

He shoved her head back into the tub, this time until her head hit the bottom between his legs. Her tube top slipped to her waist and her fat ass was sticking up in the air as her feet kicked against the tiled floor. One of Heidi's hands clasped onto Croak's bandaged shoulder and she jammed her thumb through the gauze and into the bullet wound. It felt like pushing a finger into a peanut butter and jelly sandwich.

Croak howled in pain and grabbed her wrist with his free hand and pulled her bloody thumb away. The rest of her body was still thrashing and squirming, showering the walls and floor with water. She couldn't fight his strength as he held her head pressed to the tub bottom, and her lungs burned for air and she realized she could die right here, right now. She didn't want to die, there was still so much she hadn't done in life. She wanted to live.

Heidi turned her head and slid it along the bottom of the tub and jammed her face into Croak's crotch. Her teeth clamped down on his ball sack. Croak screamed like a little girl and jerked Heidi's head out of his crotch and out of the water. A flap of skin with his pubes was hanging from her mouth and the tub water was turning pink.

"You fucking bitch!" he yelled as she pulled away from him and fell to the floor between the tub and toilet.

"What did you think would happen?" Heidi yelled, brushing the skin from her mouth and wiping water and tears from her eyes.

"What did you think would happen?" Croak growled as he jumped out of the tub and attacked her, watery blood pouring down his thigh and shoulder. Heidi screamed, but not for long.

V

"Why were you gone so long?" Renae asked Duncan in a whisper. He was lying on his back on the second motel bed, naked and under the covers. Renae had slipped under the covers beside him, resting her hand on his chest.

"I had to take care of some things. Think about some things."

"I'm sorry if I hurt your feelings."

"You don't need to apologize. We're all dealing with a lot. I'm sorry about your roommate."

"I still can't believe it," Renae said and put her head on his chest as Duncan stroked her hair. After a while she asked, "Can we drive Kiki to the bus station in the morning?"

"Of course."

"And then go far away for awhile."

"Yes. Do you still want to go to Disney World?"

"I don't know. I don't think I'm in the mood for that anymore. Is that okay? I mean, if you want to go--"

"That's okay, baby. Whatever you want."

"I don't know what I want."

Part 11

Along For The Ride

I

"I want a triple Gordy burger with cheese and bacon, a single Gordy with cheese, extra pickles, two large fries, a large Coke and a chocolate shake."

"Anything else?"

Duncan turned away from the intercom speaker and looked at Renae sitting in the passenger seat of the Terrain. She shook her head and smiled.

"That's it," Duncan said to the intercom.

"Pull ahead to the first window."

Duncan pressed the window up button to shut out the rain that was coming down in sheets. "Do we have a towel or something?" he asked. "My face and arm got drenched."

"The towels are packed away in the back," Renae said. "Come here."

Renae was wearing two loose tank tops, a white one over a pink one, and she was lifting up the front of them to offer as a towel. Duncan bent down, his eyes on her perky breasts that became exposed as she wiped his face and arm. As she reached across him, he gave the underside of one of her breasts a kiss.

She sat back in her seat as she pulled her damp shirt down and pointed out the windshield. There was a fifteen foot gap from the car ahead of them now in the drive thru line at Gordy's Superburger.

"I could have done that with my shirt," Duncan said as he inched the SUV forward.

"Your shirt's wet. Plus, it wouldn't have been as much fun."

"You are so right," Duncan said and gave her a big smile which she returned. He was glad to see her lightening up after their almost four hour trip since they'd dropped Kiki off at the bus station around noon. Duncan had stayed in the truck while Renae and Kiki had gone into the bus depot; he wasn't letting the money out of his sight, which was secure in the large leather duffel bag with the rest of their luggage and shopping spree goods behind the second row of seats. He'd remained mostly silent, giving the ladies their space as they talked and cried and made promises to see each other soon. Renae stayed with Kiki until the bus came, they hugged and cried, and when Renae returned to the SUV she was quiet and morose. Duncan had tried a little small talk but then had turned the radio on and let her be with her thoughts and feelings.

"I usually am," she said.

"Are you now?" Duncan asked as he pulled the truck up another spot in the drive thru line, now one car away from the service window.

"Except when I'm not."

Duncan reached over and playfully pinched her side causing her to squirm away and squeal. He'd found out she was quite ticklish and he enjoyed making her squeal.

"I'm glad you're doing better," Duncan said, resting his hand on her bare thigh. She was wearing white short shorts with pink trim around the waist and down the sides of the legs.

"A little," she said.

As Duncan pulled up to the drive thru window and paid the worker, Renae looked through the windshield at the two lane highway that ran in front of Gordy's. The sky was dark gray and the rain wasn't letting up. Every now and then a rumble of thunder rolled across the clouds. Just past the parking lot of the burger joint were two kids, a boy and a girl, standing next to a light post with backpacks at their feet. The boy was holding a cardboard sign that Renae couldn't read.

"Here," Duncan said, handing Renae the drinks and then putting the bag of food in his lap. He put up his window and drove toward the highway, steering with one hand while digging in the food bag with the other. "Here," he said, handing her a burger. Duncan put on his right blinker and turned onto the highway.

Renae looked at the two kids who looked like drowned rats, their clothing soaked and plastered to their bodies. The boy's sign was barely legible, the cardboard sagging and the ink running down in lines: 'Miami Maxima or Bust' it read.

Duncan pulled his burger out of the bag and then set the bag on the center console. "The fries are all spilled," he said.

"We can't just leave them like that," Renae said.

"Leave who?" Duncan asked as he unwrapped his triple burger.

"Those two kids." Her burger sat unwrapped and untouched on her thigh.

"Wha' kids?" he asked through a mouthful of American goodness.

"They were hitchhiking back in front of the restaurant."

Duncan looked in the rearview mirror and then the passenger side view mirror. He could faintly see the two figures in the distance getting smaller and smaller.

"Don't you know how dangerous it is picking up hitchhikers?" Duncan asked.

"Duncan, they were just kids."

"Probably runaways, which could mean the cops are looking for them and bring heat on us."

"They're going to Miami, same as us. And it's not like we don't have the room."

"You really want to pick up some strangers?"

Renae nodded her head and gave Duncan her winning puppy dog look. "I've been stranded before and it's not fun. Especially in the rain."

"Okay, but if they axe us to death I'll never forgive you."

II

"Oh, please forgive us," the young girl said, "we're dripping all over your truck." She was wearing black Capri pants and a red V neck t-shirt with the name Halsey on the front. Duncan's eyes were drawn more to what was behind the letters as the soaked shirt was plastered to her like a second skin and left little to the imagination, especially with her nipples practically tearing a hole through the fabric. She had platinum blonde hair that wasn't much more than an inch long.

"You're shivering, you poor things," Renae said. "Do you have a towel in your bags?"

"No," the boy said. He was in the seat behind Duncan and wearing black jeans and a purple and green t-shirt that read Arctic Monkeys on the front. His dark brown hair hung to his shoulders, water dripping from it like a leaky faucet.

"We've got some in one of our bags in the back," Renae said.

The guy turned around in his seat. "Back here?" he asked, his hand reaching toward the big brown duffel bag.

"No!" both Duncan and Renae said at the same time as Duncan watched in the rearview mirror and Renae over her shoulder.

"Here, I'll find them," Renae told them and began to lean over the front seat and stretched out her body between the kids to reach over the second row of seats.

Duncan took his eyes off the highway they were cruising down to look at Renae's long tanned legs that were stretched out. Through one of the leg holes of her shorts he could see a glimpse of her beautiful pussy and it made his crotch stir. He slid his right hand up the back of her knee and then to her thigh. Her skin was hot beneath his hand.

"Hey, I'm working here," she said and looked over her shoulder at him.

Duncan smiled and said, "I'm making sure you don't fall."

"Sure you are."

The girl in the backseat laughed and the boy smiled and stayed still as Renae's boob rubbed against his shoulder as she dug around in the bags. She found the beach towels she was looking for and pulled them out, handing one to the girl and the second to the boy. As she twisted and turned he could see down the front of her tank tops almost to her nipples and his wet pants clung to him even tighter.

"Okay, help me back," Renae said as she tried to back up. Duncan slid his hand into a leg hole of her shorts and grasped her ass cheek. "That's not helping," she said.

"Are you sure?"

The girl laughed again as she was wiping herself with the towel. The boy was holding his towel in his lap covering his woody as he noticed Renae's nipples pushing through the fabric of her tank tops. As Renae backed into the front seat the boy noticed his girlfriend's rock hard nipples and he wanted desperately to rub his aching cock.

"You should really get out of those wet clothes," Renae suggested. "Your stuff in your backpacks is dry, right?"

"Oh yeah," the girl said as she opened her pack and pulled out a short summer dress that had pictures of lily pads on it. She looked at Renae and asked, "Is it alright if I, you know, change?"

"Absolutely."

Duncan was thinking the exact same thing as he looked in the rearview mirror as the red Halsey shirt was peeled over the girl's head, her firm, well rounded breasts damp beneath the fabric, her nipples pink and stiff like pencil erasers.

"The road's that way," Renae said to Duncan who blushed and pulled his eyes away from the mirror. "I'm just kidding," she said and patted his thigh. She felt his chubby. She looked at him and raised her eyebrows and Duncan got even redder. "She is cute, isn't she?"

"Yeah," Duncan said, his voice low. "But you're beautiful."

Renae smiled and said, "Nice save." She gave his now fully rigid cock a little rub through the fabric of his Dockers as she leaned over and gave him a kiss on the cheek. "You know I'm not the jealous type."

"I know," he said, feeling her hard nipples brushing his arm through the fabric of her tank tops.

The girl had slipped on her dress and her clothes lay in a heap on the floorboard. The boy had dried off but remained in his clothes with the towel back in his lap.

"You're not going to change," the girl asked him.

"Um, no, I'm alright."

"Are you done with your towel?"

"No, I'll hold it."

III

"Hold it, what was that?" Renae asked.

"That was them."

"Zoe or Frank?"

"I don't know. Both, I think."

"What do you think they're doing?"

"Isn't that obvious? The same as us," Duncan said. He was laying on his back and Renae was on top of him, her tits resting on his chest and her pussy clamped over his stiff cock.

"I know that, but I mean what position do you think they're doing it in to be making such sounds?"

"That's seriously what you're thinking about?"

"Sure," Renae said in all seriousness. "Aren't you?"

"Well now I am." He pictured their two skinny bodies in the next room naked on the bed in the same position as them,

143

Zoe's perfectly round, firm eighteen year old breasts pressing against Frank's skinny, pale chest.

"I think he's got a big one," Renae said. "A lot of those tall, skinny guys do. Like rock stars. Did you ever see Tommy Lee's?"

"You slept with Tommy Lee?"

"No, but I saw the sex video."

"I guess I missed that."

"Did you ever. He had a huge one."

"How did we get on this topic?" Duncan asked.

"Yours is very nice, too," Renae said and resumed sliding her pussy slowly up and down the length of his shaft, her tits wiggling against his chest.

"Nice?" He thrust his hips up into her.

"Very nice."

He thrust again, harder.

"Very, very nice."

Duncan's hands were caressing Renae's ass cheeks and now he grabbed them and spread them apart as he jerked his hips harder and faster into Renae's pussy.

"Oh baby," she moaned and then put her mouth over his, her tongue flicking into his mouth almost as fast as his cock was flicking into her pussy. Duncan's mouth wrapped around her tongue, then her lips. She made whimpering noises that began to rise in tempo as Duncan kept fucking furiously beneath her. The dam broke inside her and the orgasms flooded through her pussy, her stomach, her legs.

"Oh Duncan. Oh. Oh." Another wave washed through her.

Duncan's hips were a flurry of motion, his head raised off the pillow and pressing against Renae's shoulder as the pressure in his loins grew. His fingers dug into her ass cheeks and then the thick fluid was surging through his cock and blasting into Renae's glorious love hole as his hips quivered and jerked against her until he had fully unleashed himself. His head collapsed back to the pillow.

Renae collapsed atop him, her breathing heavy, small spasms causing her hips and legs to flinch. She could feel his heart pounding through his chest and she kissed his neck and face. He wrapped his arms around her and hugged her body tightly to his.

They heard the door open and then close next door.

"They must have finished about the same time we did," Renae said. She started to move off of him, but he held her tight.

"Where are you going?" Duncan said.

"I thought I might be squishing you."

"You and what army. You feel good."

"You, too," she said and snuggled against him. "Can you reach the sheet?"

He stretched a hand searching for the sheet and then felt his semi hard cock began to slip out of Renae's pussy. He pushed his pelvis upwards and at the same time felt her pussy muscles clench onto him.

"You're not going anywhere," she said.

"Nice catch."

He kissed her as he pulled the sheet over her back and then they drifted to sleep still attached.

IV

Duncan thought he was dreaming at first, that he was in a jungle or zoo. Then he heard Renae's voice, "Oh my god, he sounds like a monkey."

"How do you know it's him?"

Renae laughed, causing Duncan's limp dick to pop out of her. "That was your fault," she told him.

"He does sound like a monkey."

The both laughed, and then made imitation whispering monkey noises that made them laugh more.

"I need something to drink," Duncan said.

"Want me to go get you something?"

145

Duncan rolled her off him and said, "No, you work on your monkey impressions, I'll go get us some sodas." He put on his pants and slid some change and the room key off a night stand.

"Hurry back with your banana," she told him.

The vending machines were in an alcove three doors past Zoe and Frank's room. On the other side of the vending machine alcove was an outdoor pool area with a dozen lounge chairs all surrounded by a waist high chain link fence. It was closed after hours but Duncan could see a shape sitting on one of the chairs. There was a glow coming from the pool lights and for a moment Duncan thought the shape could be Frank, but he knew that wasn't possible.

Duncan grabbed a Dr. Pepper and a 7Up and walked back toward the room. Zoe and Frank's door opened and Frank bumped into Duncan. But it wasn't Frank. Not unless Frank had lost all his hair, gained a hundred pounds and aged at least thirty years.

"Oh, sorry," the man said. His 'oh' sounded like that of a monkey's. Behind the man, through the open motel door, Duncan saw Zoe, naked, climbing out of the bed. "Excuse me," the man said and walked quickly to a blue Buick parked in front of the room.

As the car drove away Duncan walked to his motel room and put the key in the door. Frank, the real Frank, was trotting from the pool area toward the rooms. "It's not what you think," he said. Duncan stepped into his room and shut the door.

Renae was sitting up against the headboard and Duncan approached her and gave her the Dr. Pepper. "Everything alright?" she asked.

"You're not going to believe this."

"What?" Renae looked worried.

"That little girl is turning tricks next door."

"And?" she said, no longer looking worried.

"And...well...." He suddenly realized his hypocrisy.

"You didn't have a problem a week ago when you were buying."

"No, you're right," he said.

She set her soda on the nightstand and looked at him. "What if I wanted to turn tricks right now?"

"You don't need to. We have plenty of money."

"Not real money. And it's not always about money."

"Everything's about money."

"Maybe for you."

V

Duncan awoke to an empty bed and looked at the clock on the nightstand that read: 10:51. He laid there for another minute seeing if he could hear Renae in the bathroom, but all was silent. He got out of bed and did some stretches of his sore back as he walked to the motel's curtained window and pulled it aside enough to look outside but not expose his nakedness. The day was bright and the Terrain was sitting in front of the room but there was no one around.

Duncan got dressed and put on his shoes. He looked around for the room key but it was missing. Obviously Renae had taken it so she could get back in, but he wondered where she had gone. Maybe she was getting them breakfast or had gone down to the vending machines for a soda.

He glanced at the clock again and it was now a minute past eleven and they were supposed to be checking out of their room. He began putting things in their suitcases, which was practically nothing of his but Renae had clothes all over the place and about every inch of bathroom counter space was taken up with make-up, lotions, body sprays and hair care products. When he finished packing it was 11:21, and still no sign of Renae returning to the room.

He propped the motel door open with one of his suitcases and knocked on Frank and Zoe's door. There was no answer. He looked around the parking lot but it only had another car in it parked near the office. A few cars went by on the road in front of the motel but he didn't see any people

147

anywhere. But then he heard laughter coming from around the corner of the building, just past the vending machines.

Duncan walked that way, glancing over his shoulder at his propped open motel room to make sure no one had magically appeared to try to rob him. It was nerve wracking having such a large quantity of cash on hand and constantly worrying that someone might try to take it. He couldn't remember any time in his past where he'd ever been concerned about anything of his being stolen or that he had to fear being robbed, not to mention now the added risk of police and criminals after him. He had maybe bitten off more than he could chew but it was too late now to fix it. He had to keep going forward while constantly looking over his shoulder.

"Hey, what are you doing?" Duncan asked. He stood at the fence overlooking the pool area. Renae and Zoe were laid out on side by side lounge chairs facing the sun, their backs to Duncan. From his angle Duncan could see their legs and small patches of bikini - Renae's white and Zoe's black. Renae had more of a tan and her toe nails were perfectly manicured with red polish whereas Zoe's toes had chipped pink polish and her skin tone was more white.

Renae turned in her seat and looked at Duncan through her Gucci sunglasses. Duncan's eyes were drawn to her beautiful breasts in the white bikini top, her nipples shadowing the fabric.

"It's check out time," Duncan said. "I got everything--"

"We want to stay," Renae interrupted.

"Stay?"

Zoe turned in her lounge chair, her breasts testing the fabric of her bikini top and almost touching Renae's breasts as she looked at Duncan through a pair of cheap gas station sunglasses. "Go get your swim suit," Zoe said. "Join us."

"Let's just relax and have a day by the pool," Renae said. "It's not like there's anywhere we need to be."

"At least not for two days," Zoe added.

"Watch this," Frank said and the girls turned to watch him run to the pool's edge in his red trunks and he jumped and

148

did a half twist in the air and dove into the water backwards. Zoe clapped.

Renae turned back to Duncan. "Well?"

"I'll check in at the desk and then get my suit."

VI

"The guy was wearing a suit, so I knew he had money," Renae said to Zoe. They were floating in the water as they hung onto the edge of the pool and Renae had been filling Zoe in on the finer arts of the escort business for the past two hours. They had all played in the water a bit and now Duncan had left to get some sodas and chips and Frank was asleep face down on his towel on top of one of the lounge chairs. "But just because they have money doesn't mean that they're normal."

"What do you mean?" Zoe asked.

"I mean that just because they have money doesn't mean they can do anything they want and just because they dress nice doesn't mean that they might not be fucked up in the head. You gotta remember that you're in charge, they're paying you for your services and you say what goes or does not go."

Zoe nodded her head.

Renae continued. "If you're not clear up front some of these guys will take it for granted that you'll do anything."

"I don't like it in the ass," Zoe said.

"Then tell them that's off limits. Make sure everything is clear up front."

"I mean, I've never done it in the ass, but my ass is so little I don't think I'd like it."

"Don't knock it till you try it. But don't let a customer be your first for something like that. Try it with Frank or someone you trust first."

"I trust Frank. He's good to me."

"He seems like a good guy. Usually boyfriends don't last long when you're an escort."

"I told a guy I didn't want to suck his balls because they smelled like dirty gym socks and this fatso tried to push my head down there. Well I screamed and Frank was right there and had a knife to the guy's throat. Frank always has a knife. We took that guy's wallet and his car." Zoe laughed. "Frank says I should have a knife, but I don't know."

Renae shook her head. "It's better to just try to avoid people like that if you can. Having a knife doesn't help you unless you know how to use it and are ready to use it. Otherwise it's more likely to be taken away from you and used against you."

"Yeah, I don't like violence. What happened with you and the man with the suit? How was he fucked up like you said?"

Renae told her the story. She had taken an Uber to his home in north Las Vegas and he answered the door in his suit, a light gray three piece with a pocket square that matched his light purple shirt. He had a hundred dollar haircut, every strand of his silver hair in perfect place, and it was obvious he was the boss in whatever business he did. Renae thought he was handsome, though she wouldn't ever have dated someone like him because he was a couple inches shorter than her. But this wasn't a date, this was business.

"Hi, I'm Fantasia," she said as soon as he'd opened the door and invited her in. "Do you mind if I freshen up?"

"No," he said.

"Okay, where is your--"

"No, I mean I do mind." he told her and held up a hand to stop her. "I want you to get undressed right here."

"I'd feel more comfortable--"

"Sh!" he said and pulled an envelope out of his inside breast pocket and handed it to her.

Renae didn't like how this was starting out but when she looked inside the envelope it contained three times the amount she had told him on the phone. That should have been a warning to her but she was hungry for cash and still new to the game.

150

"Okay," she said, "where do--"

"Sh! From this point on do not talk any more. You've been paid and you are to do as you are told. Take off your clothes."

Renae was standing in the foyer of the upper middle class home, the businessman less than three feet in front of her watching her intently, his hands at his sides. She was wearing a tight black and gold cocktail dress that had a zipper on the right side which she proceeded to pull down. She watched the man as she slipped out of her dress and let it fall to the hardwood floor. His eyes watched her every move but never made contact with her eyes.

She stood in front of him wearing a black lace bra and panty set and open toed gold high heels. The house was warm and smelled of flowers and Old Spice after shave.

"Everything except the shoes," he told her.

Renae's arms went to her back and undid her bra and let it fall to the floor atop her dress. She bent down and slowly slid the panties off her hips and down over her shoes. As she stood back up she could see a bead of sweat on the man's forehead and it was obvious he was fully aroused. His eyes were on her little furry heart above her pussy. Renae reached for his zipper with a smile.

"No, I'm married," he said and took a step back. Renae straightened up and wondered what it was she was supposed to be doing then. "Walk upstairs," he told her and pointed to the stairs at the edge of the foyer.

Renae's heels clicked against the hardwood floor to the carpeted stairs. She began walking up the stairs, the man right behind and below her, his face inches away from her ass which she purposely gave a little more sway to with each step she took. At the top of the stairs he directed her to the master bedroom that was huge and he shut the double doors behind them.

Renae walked toward the king sized sleigh bed, but the man stopped her and said, "Over here, get on the table."

Along one wall was a fireplace and in front of it was a glass coffee table with a brass frame and legs. On the other side of the table were two large upholstered chairs that looked like they belonged in a castle. Renae wondered if he wanted her to dance on the table while he sat in one of the chairs and watched.

She approached the table and began to lift one of her feet, wobbling to keep her balance on the other.

"No, lie on the table," he told her.

"Oh, I thought--"

"Sh!"

Renae sat on the table and laid back. The glass was cold against her skin.

"Roll over," the man said.

Renae did as he requested, her breasts pressed against the glass, her calves and heels sticking out over the edge of the table.

She heard him undressing and wondered if he was going to lie of top of her, maybe fuck her from behind. She liked it that way. But instead she saw him scooting on his back underneath the table. He was completely naked except for his black socks and dress shoes. He was positioned the same direction as Renae but his head was only at her chest level. She realized he didn't have any body hair and he had a pretty good physique for an older guy. His cock was about average and was sticking straight up from his groin, the tip just a few inches from the glass of the coffee table.

The man lifted his head and began licking and kissing the glass where her nipples were. Renae wasn't sure what she was supposed to do, if she should moan or pretend she liked it or something. She kept her body still atop the glass while the man beneath her slid his tongue from her tits to her belly button and then to her pussy.

"Spread your legs," he told her breathlessly.

Renae did so until her knees were at the edges of the table. The man continued licking beneath her pussy, his mouth making slurping noises against the glass.

"Oh yeah," Renae said, trying to get into it.

"Sh!"

The man's hands were plastered to the glass on either side of his face beneath her thighs. His tongue slid back and forth and then his lips would suck on the glass.

"Now sit up," he told her.

Renae let her legs slide down either side of the coffee table and she pushed herself up with her hands so she was now straddling the man's face beneath the glass.

"Spread your lips."

Renae slid her hands to her crotch and spread her pussy, baring her pink hole to him. She watched his head moving wildly beneath the table, the glass fogging up with his breath and smeared with his saliva. Renae wasn't hating it and her pussy made some smear marks of its own on her side of the glass.

The man stopped licking at the glass and he was moving his body beneath the table until his stiff cock was lined up under Renae's pussy. She could see the precum glistening the top of his dick as he lifted his hips and pushed against the glass. Renae shifted her hips back and forth, wiggling her pussy atop the glass over his cock.

The old man groaned as he lowered his hips and then pushed them back up towards Renae's pussy. His precum left a streak on the glass as his cock thudded against it. He began to fuck the glass and Renae got into his rhythm bouncing her pussy up and down atop his shielded cock, her ass bouncing against the table top, her tits jiggling from the jarring motion. The glass actually felt sort of good on her pussy, or maybe she was just imagining it as she watched the man totally engrossed in his thrusting, his teeth clenched and eyes squinting. then his milky liquid was squirting out of his cock and creating a film on the glass underside and he continued banging his cock into the glass as he cried out. Renae bounced atop his slimy mess and then suddenly there was a loud shattering sound and she was falling though the table as glass rained down upon the man's body.

153

They both screamed in surprise and then in pain as Renae realized there was a huge chunk of glass imbedded in the back of her left thigh. The man had glass stuck in him as well and there was blood all over his cock but Renae didn't know it was her's or his.

"I was wondering how you got that scar," Duncan said, having returned to the pool with drinks and snacks halfway through the story.

"Did you call an ambulance?" Zoe asked.

"No, the man couldn't take the chance of his wife finding out," Renae said. "He gave me extra money and I went to the hospital and had to get stitches."

"How'd he explain it to his wife?" Duncan asked.

"I don't know. I never saw him again."

"Oh wow," Zoe said as she reached for some potato chips. "Was that the craziest thing that ever happened to you?"

Renae drank some Dr. Pepper and said, "No, the craziest was when a girlfriend I was with knocked a guy out and tried to steal all his money."

"How did that turn out?" Zoe asked.

Renae looked at Duncan and said, "I don't know yet."

VII

"You know," Duncan said to Renae once they'd returned to their room, "I don't care that you and Zoe are prostitutes."

"That's good," Renae replied.

"But for right now it would be better if she didn't do it because I don't want to take the chance of drawing any heat our way."

"They don't have any money, Duncan. That's how they're financing their trip to Miami Maxima."

Duncan shook his head. "Tell them we'll cover all of their expenses. They can relax and enjoy themselves and we'll give them a ride to Miami."

"The festival isn't for two more days," Renae said.

"So?"

"So tomorrow they want to go to Disney World."

Duncan sang the tune that was in his head in Oregon: "I'm going to Disney Land."

Renae smiled and corrected him. "Disney World."

Part 12

It's a Small World

I

Disney World was ridiculously huge, consisting of more than thirty resorts and hotels and nearly a dozen different parks and amusement areas as well as retail and dining complexes. It wasn't so much a city but more like a state with multiple cities. When Croak pulled off U.S. 192 following the signs to Walt Disney World Resort he was blown away by how many miles of roadways there were inside the place, not to mention monorails, a railroad and even a ferryboat transporting customers to and from the parking lots.

He had no idea where to even begin to set a trap for Duncan and Renae. There was even the slight chance that they were already at Disney World, but he doubted it unless they'd driven straight from the fiasco at Renae's aunt's house outside of Atlanta like he had. And Croak was also fully aware that they might not even come to Disney World, that he could have been feeding his ex-fiancé false information before he'd gone and stolen Croak's money and tried to disappear. Actually, Duncan would be a fool to come to Disney World.

But no matter how much of a fool Duncan might be, Croak was pretty confident that he wouldn't try to check into any of the hotels on Disney World property. That would require a driver's license and credit card and he was surely wanted by police, if not as a suspect then at least for questioning. So Croak ruled out the nearly three dozen hotels, resorts and campground and decided to focus on the parking lots.

Even so, there were multiple amusement areas spread out across the complex, as well as a couple water parks and four golf courses, not that he expected Duncan to be playing golf. After a little research and some more deductive reasoning, Croak surmised that anyone coming to Disney World for their first time would make it a point to visit Magic Kingdom Park. It was there that the magical castle seen at the beginning of every Disney film was located, as well as multiple parades throughout the day, and it contained six different amusement park areas within the attraction.

For people staying at the resorts there were monorails, busses and even a boat they could ride to reach Magic Kingdom Park. For all the tourists arriving for a day of fun and not staying overnight on the property, there were huge parking lots that were accessed by a monorail or a ferryboat to bring them to Magic Kingdom Park.

Croak settled on a spot where he could see droves of excited men, women and children in every shape, size and color. He remained in his white Toyota Camry with a huge Disney sun screen shielding his front windshield. He kept a cooler with drinks and sandwiches on the passenger seat and leaned back as far as he could in the driver's seat and still see out the side window with his binoculars.

On the first day he used up the last two travel toilets he had and then pissed in an empty bottle before the day was done. The next day he had reused two empty bottles almost three times during his stakeout. Halfway through the day he'd had to take a crap and held it as long as he could before having to find a bathroom. He figured it would be just his luck that they'd arrive while he was on a shitter. But that was why he made it a point to stay until the park closed and watched everyone go back to their cars just in case he had missed them when they arrived.

He was watching first and foremost for the maroon Mustang that would stand out among all of the newer cars coming into the lot. As for people walking to and from the parking lot he quickly discounted anyone walking with kids, which was by far the majority. Croak kept his eyes peeled for groups of two or three people, thinking that maybe the short, big titted Asian could be with them.

On the third day Croak nearly missed them because it seemed as if Duncan and Renae were with two teenagers. When Croak finally ID'd Duncan with his binoculars, the foursome was already getting onto the ferryboat. Croak had fumbled out of the car, spilling his Orange Crush and knocking his bag of tortilla chips onto the ground. He was more than two hundred yards from the ferryboat and it was departing before he made it even half the distance.

That's fine, Croak thought, they had to come back the same way. One thing was certain, they weren't carrying the stolen counterfeit money into the park with them. He spent the next two hours driving up and down the parking lot lanes looking for the Mustang. If he could find that he was sure the money would be in it because it's not like Duncan would leave it behind in a motel for some maid to find.

Croak was pissed he couldn't locate the car. He'd had visions of breaking into the vehicle and retrieving what was rightfully his and then when Duncan and his friends walked back to the car Croak could run them down with his car. He didn't care about any of them except Duncan: he had to die.

II

"I thought we were going to die," Duncan said.
"That was great!" Zoe exclaimed. "Let's do it again!"

157

"The line's too long," Frank said.

"I need a break," Renae said as she held onto Duncan's arm, Big Thunder Mountain Railroad receding behind them. "Isn't anyone else hungry?"

They had been going on rides and visiting stores and standing in lines for over four hours and they'd barely seen even a quarter of what Magic Kingdom Park had to offer.

"We've got to do Splash Mountain!" Zoe said as she pulled on Frank's hand in hers. "You promised."

Duncan looked at Renae. "You can go if you want to. I want a turkey leg we saw at that wagon around the corner."

"You guys go ahead," Duncan said to Zoe and Frank. "We'll meet you at the Country Bear Jamboree when you're done."

"Awesome!" Zoe said and pulled Frank toward the line in front of the log flume ride. "Ready to get wet?" she asked her man.

"With you, always," Frank said and brushed the back of her hand against his crotch. Zoe smiled and rubbed her body against his. "There he is again," Frank whispered in her ear.

"No way," she said and looked over her right shoulder.

"His wife is fucking clueless," Frank said, not looking directly at the overweight man wearing the yellow shorts and a t-shirt that read 'Alabama Slama.' The man was in his forties with short, light colored hair that was matched by his overweight wife in a green and white dress that reached to her fat knees. They had a portly girl in between them who looked to be about twelve and kept asking her parents questions.

They had first spotted the man two rides ago, though it was possible he'd been stalking them longer than that. The man couldn't keep his eyes off of Zoe and when she'd looked at him once a little too long he slowly licked his lips as his eyes stroked her body. At the last ride while waiting in line for the runaway train, Zoe had put her back to him and then bent over to adjust her shoe. She looked behind her as she did so and made eye contact with the fat man. He rubbed his crotch and smiled as he looked into her eyes.

"Do you think he's got much money?" Zoe asked Frank as they got onto the log flume.

"As expensive as this place is, I'd think he'd have to."

Zoe looked over and blew the fat man a kiss as the ride took off. The fat man smiled and she could see a little bulge in the front of his shorts.

Minutes later they exited the ride, Zoe and Frank both soaked. Zoe was wearing a short, white skirt and blouse and both had become transparent and showed the outlines of her bra and panties beneath. Many others were coming off the ride all wet as well and Zoe stood by the corner of a restroom dripping with water as she awaited her trick. The fat man and his family were not far behind and he spotted her immediately. Zoe motioned with her head to him and then walked into a bathroom that read 'Family Restroom, Baby Changing Stations.'

There was no one else in the bathroom and it had four oversized stalls, each with a toilet and a plastic counter attached to the wall that had seatbelt straps for placing an infant in. Zoe entered the farthest stall from the entrance and left the door unlatched behind her. She removed her wet blouse and set it on the plastic counter.

"Hi," the nervous voice behind her said. The man's voice wasn't very deep and when Zoe turned to look at him she could see his hands trembling. His yellow shorts were wet, she assumed from the ride, and poking out in front of him like a pup tent. He was breathing heavy through his open mouth, his eyes glued to Zoe's wet cotton bra that her nipples and areola could be seen through.

"I got so wet on that ride," Zoe said as she stood demurely not more than an arm's length away. "Do you want to feel how wet I am?"

The fat man nodded like a Bobblehead doll.

"Do you have any money?"

"What?" The man looked confused. "Are you, like, a prostitute?"

Zoe dramatically snatched her shirt off the counter and put it over her breasts. "What!? How rude!"

"No, no, I'm sorry," the man quickly said as he put up his hands to stop her. "I didn't mean that."

"I'm just a girl that likes to have fun," Zoe said. "And it's not cheap having fun here."

"Ain't that the truth," the man said. "I can't believe--"

The man froze and his eyes grew wide when he heard another voice enter the bathroom. "I don't think anyone's in here, mommy," the young girl's voice said. "Okay, I will." They heard the sound of a stall door closing and then the sound of peeing.

Zoe stepped close to the fat man, her tits rubbing against his t-shirt. She slipped her right hand into the front of his shorts, having to struggle to get past his waistband, and was then holding his small boner in her hand.

The man leaned forward to kiss her but Zoe put her left hand up to block him. They heard a toilet flush and then the water in a sink running and then the girl's voice as she ran out of the bathroom door, "Mommy, can we do the--"

"I really do need some spending cash," Zoe said softly, her hand squeezing the man's sticky erection in his shorts.

"Doesn't your boyfriend have money?"

"He's not my boyfriend. Why would I be in here if I had a boyfriend?"

"Oh yeah, I guess so," the man said getting lost in the feel of her hand that was so soft and so warm around his pointy prick. He put one of his meaty hands on Zoe's firm, voluptuous breast, feeling her nipple through the wet fabric.

"Are you going to pay me?" Zoe asked.

"Uh-huh," the man groaned as his other hand lifted her skirt and touched her pussy through the fabric of her cotton panties. "How old are you?" he asked.

"Does it matter?" she replied as she tried to stroke his cock but his tight waistband was restricting her.

"No," he said, "it doesn't matter." He pulled her panties aside and pushed a finger inside her.

"Ooh," Zoe said. She struggled with her left hand to undo the clasp on his shorts and then she was pushing them and his red and white boxers with lobsters on them to his ankles. His hard cock wasn't much more than four inches long and Zoe stroked it vigorously.

The man had two fingers sliding and feeling around in Zoe's pussy and his other hand pushed the fabric away from one of her tits and his thumb pressed against her pretty pink nipple. Zoe's right hand stroked the fat man's tiny weenie and her left hand was juggling his balls.

Underneath that action Zoe saw Frank's hand sliding beneath the bathroom stall door and reaching for the man's wallet in his shorts that were around his fat ankles.

"Oh yeah, that's good," Zoe said as she pushed her pelvis against the man's hand. She jerked him off faster and harder.

"Oh!" he said as he felt the surge, but at the same time he felt something tugging at his feet. "Hey!"

The fat man's cock slipped from Zoe's hand as he twisted his body, his sperm spitting out a stream against the bathroom stall wall. The man bent down to grab at the hand that was trying to pull his wallet from his buttoned back pocket. Zoe shoved the man hard and he hit the stall door, popping it open. He couldn't get his footing due to the shorts and underwear at his feet and he sprawled on top of Frank who had been on his hands and knees.

"Aaughh!" Frank howled when the half naked man landed atop him.

"I saw you!" the fat man yelled. "I'm calling the police."

"Get off him," Zoe yelled, pushing at the fat man whose cock and balls were atop Frank's head. "We'll tell your wife."

"I don't care," the fat man said as Frank struggled and squirmed beneath him. "You little thieves are going to jail."

"We're not thieves," Frank said and managed to pull a hundred dollar bill from his shirt pocket and wave it at the man who was sprawled atop his back. "See, we've got money!"

"You probably stole that, too," the man said and snatched it out of Frank's hand.

161

"Get off me!" Frank yelled.

"Oh no you don't," the fat man said, keeping Frank pinned to the floor, the weight of his stomach on Frank's back and the fat man's groin on the back of Frank's head. The fat man bent his knees to be able to reach the cell phone in his shorts pocket. Before he could unlock the phone, Zoe kicked it out of his hand and it skittered across the bathroom floor.

"You little bitch!" the man yelled and punched Zoe in the leg.

"Ow!" Zoe cried.

"Don't you hurt her!" Frank roared and he shifted his weight enough to get his hand to his pants pocket. He pulled out his pocket knife and flicked the blade open and rammed it in the side of one of fat man's ass cheeks atop his head.

The man squealed like a pig. Frank jabbed him in the ass again with his knife and this time the fat man rolled off of him. Frank scurried away from the man who was whimpering and crying as he tried to put his hands over the two punctures in his ass cheeks. Blood pooled beneath him on the black and white tiles.

Zoe grabbed her shirt and jumped over the bleeding man and helped Frank up. As they ran out of the bathroom, Frank laughed and said, "That didn't go as planned."

III

Croak hadn't planned on them returning on the ferryboat so soon. He'd only been paying half attention as he looked through the binoculars at the crowd of people exiting the craft. His eyes were actually glued to a pair of black and blue tiger striped Spandex pants pasted to a Kim Kardashian type ass. Now that's something he could really get into, he thought, a woman with serious meat on her bones. It reminded Croak that he was getting hungry.

That's when he saw the huge half eaten turkey leg in some woman's hand, but she wasn't eating it. Instead she was being pulled by her other hand by a man moving quickly past everyone getting off the ferryboat. And behind them, moving just as quickly, were the two teenagers he'd seen earlier. Croak couldn't believe Duncan and Renae were leaving the park already.

He started the Camry and pulled slowly out of the parking spot he'd been in the past couple of hours. As much as he'd like to gun the engine and run over Duncan and anyone else in his way as they speed walked down the middle of one of the lanes, Croak kept his cool. He wanted to find out which car was theirs first, because obviously they were no longer in the Mustang.

Croak turned down the lane that they were walking. He was about thirty yards behind them and there were two other families walking down the same lane.

"Look out," a mother said to her two boys as the Camry slowly creeped by, "stay to the side."

Croak ignored everything except for the foursome. Suddenly they cut between two sets of vehicles and into another lane. Croak wondered if he'd been seen.

IV

"He's right there," Frank said, panic in his voice.

"Just be cool," Duncan said. "He probably has no idea who we are."

Renae tugged on Duncan's hand. "Slow down and act natural." She glanced casually over her shoulder at the white security truck that was heading their way down the lane. "He's not even looking at us."

The four of them reached the beige SUV. The security truck was only three cars away and slowly moving closer.

"Oh shit," Frank said, "we're screwed."

Zoe pushed Frank's back against the side of the GMC Terrain and then she pressed her body against him and, taking his face in her hands, began kissing him deeply. Frank's hands slid up her sides and then wrapped around her back as his mouth opened and Zoe's tongue pushed into him. He stuck his tongue into her and something else of his began to harden and press into her body.

"Get in the truck," Duncan said. He and Renae were already sitting in the front seats and Duncan had started the truck. He wasn't sure what he would have done if the security truck had stopped behind them; he imagined ramming the truck and racing away but he doubted it would be that easy.

What pissed him off the most was that he didn't even know why they were running away. He and Renae had been sitting in Country Bear Jamboree enjoying the singing bears when Zoe and Frank had rushed in and said they had to go. Duncan could see the fear on their faces and there was blood on Frank's hand. Renae had handed him some napkins and shushed them when they tried to explain, telling them to wait until they got to the truck.

"What the fuck's going on?" Duncan growled as soon as the two teenagers were in the Terrain and he was pulling out of the parking space. His attention was on the security truck and he didn't see the white Camry following him down the lane and out of the parking lot. He also had no clue that the security truck had just saved his life...for now.

Frank stammered, "I, uh..."

"Some old guy tried to molest me in the bathroom," Zoe said.

"Oh my god," Renae said, turning in her seat to face Zoe behind her. "Are you okay?"

Zoe nodded. "Frank heard me scream and when he ran into the bathroom, the guy jumped on top of Frank."

"Why would he jump on Frank?" Duncan asked.

"I don't know," Zoe said, "the guy was psycho. He stuck his hand in me."

"I stabbed him," Frank said. "In the ass. I wasn't trying to hurt him. I just did it so Zoe could get away."

"Are you okay?" Renae asked, looking at the two teenagers. She looked at Frank and asked, "What's that white stuff on your shirt and in your hair?"

"Um," he said, patting some of the sticky substance away.

"It's from the log flume ride," Zoe lied. "I had got some on me, too. Kinda gross."

"Ew," Renae said.

Duncan turned his attention to the road and was glad they made it to the highway without incident. Croak followed them heading south, staying a few car lengths behind, waiting for his opportunity to make a move.

V

Taggart made a move, but he couldn't believe how nervous he felt. He never felt nervous like this when he hit on strippers, but this was no stripper sitting beside him on the green fabric couch. She was a thirty six year old graphic designer who had her own successful business and who'd had more college than Taggart. Her auburn colored hair hung down in wavy curls to rest atop the bulge of her breasts. She was wearing a light brown sweater that almost matched her eyes and a pair of dark grey pants and sensible black shoes with no heels.

They were watching a sit-com rerun on the TV in front of them and he couldn't remember which of them had even turned it on when they'd entered the room. But right now, Taggart was trying to remember to breathe as his heart beat faster and sweat rolled down from his armpits under his shirt. He felt like a teenager again as he bit his lower lip and gently placed his left hand on the woman's thigh.

She looked at him and asked, "Gary, what are you doing?"

He swallowed and his instinct told him to pull his hand back but he left if on her warm, firm thigh. He could tell she'd been keeping up with her strenuous workout routines. He gave her a light squeeze.

"I've missed you, Angie," he said looking into her eyes.

"Have you?"

"I really have."

Her hand went to his and she gave it a squeeze and then removed it from her thigh and set it on the couch between them. "I didn't tell Cassie or the boys that you'd been shot."

"That's good," Taggart said as he looked down at her hand atop his. Her nails were short and unpolished, nothing like all of the acrylic nails he was so used to looking at in the clubs. "I should probably see them and tell them in person so they know I'm okay."

"So it takes you getting shot to want to see your kids?" Angie asked.

"That's not fair, Angie. I don't see them because you took them halfway across the country."

"I didn't think you'd miss them. You were never home."

"My work--"

"Bullshit, Gary," his wife said, her voice rising. "Your office isn't in a strip club."

"Actually, this case I'm on right now--"

"I don't want to hear it. I hate your job, always have, and then when you moved us all to that god forsaken desert--"

"It's where the department posted me."

"You don't need to do that kind of work," Angie said. "I can support us with my business."

"Oh, and what, be a house husband?" Taggart shook his head. "I'm good at what I do. The best."

"You could be good at anything you set your mind to." Angie stood up from the couch and Taggart grabbed her hand.

"I am good at something else," he said.

"What?" She saw his eyes go to her crotch. "Are you serious?" She pulled her hand but Taggart hung on to it.

"Why did you come here?" he asked.

"I get a call my husband has been shot, of course I'm going to come."

Taggart smiled.

"What?" she asked.

"I like when you come."

"Would you stop it?" she said and pulled her arm again but couldn't get loose. "Will you let me go?"

"No."

"What do you mean no?"

"I let you go nine months ago and I've regretted it every night since."

"Good."

"No, not good. It's been bad. I miss you and the kids."

"They've missed you too."

"Just them?"

"I miss you too, sometimes."

"Just sometimes?"

"Gary, what do you want me to say?"

Gary shook his head. "It's not what I want you to say. It's what I need to say. When you walked into the hospital room it was like I was an empty vase and as soon as I saw you I was filled full. I've been empty ever since you left but with you here right now, I don't feel empty. I don't want to be empty. I need you, Angie. I want you. I love you."

"Don't do this," she said, her voice barely a whisper.

"I have to. I should have done it months ago. Come back to me."

She shook her head as tears rolled down her cheeks. "The boys have started school. Cassie has already made friends. We're staying in Ohio."

"Okay, what if I come to Ohio?"

"I don't know."

Her hand was sweaty in his grip but he wouldn't let her go as he looked into her wet, brown eyes. "Angie, I want to be with you."

"You say that now--"

"And I mean it."

"But your job always becomes more important."

"Not anymore. Let's just try. Do you still love me?"

She wiped at her tears with her sweater sleeve. "That's a dumb question. Of course I do. I don't know how not to love you."

"I feel the same way," he said as he stood up.

Angie started to say something else but Taggart stole her words with a kiss. His mouth hungrily invaded hers and she accepted him, reluctant at first but then a wall crumbled and she pressed up against him. Her free hand went to his right shoulder and he flinched. "Oh, I'm sorry," she said, a pained look on her face.

"No, I'm sorry," he told her and led her to the bedroom of the hotel suite the agency had put him up in.

They delicately undressed each other, hands sliding over one another's bodies that they knew better than anyone else's. Taggart laid her on the bed and then positioned his head between her legs. He smiled when he felt how smooth her thighs were, knowing that she'd shaved before going to see him at the hospital.

Her pussy lips were pink and moist, looking like a flower that had bloomed. He moved his mouth between her legs and she moaned as her feet raised in the air. Taggart kept his weight on his left arm, his left hand cupping his wife's ass cheek and his tongue slid up and down, parting her pussy even more and then nuzzling the flat of his tongue against her stiff clit. Angie moaned louder as her hands palmed the back of her husband's bald head.

He licked and sucked on her pussy until she was shoving it against his face and crying out in orgasmic bliss. "Oh, you are so good at that," Angie panted. "The best."

"I had a good teacher," Taggart said as he rose up on the bed between Angie's outstretched quivering legs. His stiff cock was leading the way in front of him and he sunk it into her hot, pink hole.

"Oh god!" they both exclaimed at the same time as his thick cock filled her completely. His left hand slid up her torso and he grabbed her heaving breast as his hips moved slowly back and forth. Angie propped herself up on her elbows and

168

looked down at her husband's cock moving in and out of her. She liked watching his veiny manhood glistening with her juices as he fucked her. Taggart smiled as he tugged on her pebble hard nipple and she cried out as jolts of pleasurable pain shot from her nipple to her pussy.

Angie let her head flop back onto the pillows as her husband fucked her harder and faster, his grunts filling the room and punctuated by her panting screams. Taggart had fucked a lot of women, but none were ever as good as with the woman he loved and knew so intimately. His cock rammed in and out of her, his balls smacking against her ass cheeks, his fingers tugging on her nipple like he was pulling apart taffy. She screamed in delight as he blew his load deep inside her, his cock squirting and squirting like it was never going to stop until finally he collapsed atop her in a sweaty heap. She wrapped her arms around her husband and he ignored the shooting pain in his right shoulder.

Taggart awoke to the phone ringing and instinctively went for it with his right hand. He cringed in pain and spat out a swear word. Angie was naked in the bed next to him her leg entangled through his, her pussy pressed against his hip. He grabbed the phone with his left hand.

"You're going to like this," the voice on the other end said.

Taggart did like it, but when he looked at his wife lying beside him he knew she wouldn't like it one bit.

VI

"You're goddamn right I don't like it!" the head of Disney security, Toby Crestly, said. "Do you have any idea the kind of stress we deal with here having to worry about goddamn terrorists and mass shootings and suicide bombers? We almost put the whole park on lockdown. Do you have any idea what a clusterfuck that would cause and how much money our shareholders would lose every hour we're out of operation?"

"But that didn't happen, right?" Taggart asked the smaller man that reminded him of the spitting and sputtering cartoon character Yosemite Sam.

"Goddamn right it didn't happen because we are professionals. And that's how we caught this funny money so fast as well."

Taggart had already looked at the half a dozen counterfeit hundreds on the table. Taggart brought up the Average Joe photo on his phone and showed it to Crestly. "And you're certain this isn't the man that you're stabbing victim got the hundred dollar bill from?"

"Does that look like a kid? No, I told you he was a teenager. And he was seen with a teenage girl."

Still holding his phone up, Taggart asked, "Is there any way to check if this image is anywhere in your camera footage? In Vegas they can--"

"Our system is better than Vegas," Crestly bragged. He took Taggart's phone and handed it to one of his security techs who in turn Bluetoothed it to the system. He handed Taggart back his phone. Within minutes they were looking at video footage of the Average Joe, Renae Savoy, and the two teenagers, one of whom had stabbed another Disney guest.

"Can you track them to the parking lot?" Taggart asked.

"We can track them all the way to the goddamn freeway," Crestly bellowed.

"There!" Taggart said. "Get me a copy of that license plate."

The security tech hit a couple of keys and a printer spit out the GMC Terrain's picture.

Taggart made a couple phone calls and when he was done he smiled at Crestly and said, "Every cop in the state will be looking for them."

Part 13

Miami Maxima

I

"Every cop in the state is here," Duncan said as he pulled in front of the office of the Manta Ray Motel. "We should go to another motel."

"Duncan, there is no other motel," Renae said. "I checked online at more than thirty places. This is it."

"People have been booking hotels for months in advance to go to Miami Maxima," Zoe said from the backseat.

"Do you really think the cops are looking for us?" Frank asked worriedly.

"No," Duncan said. At least not for you, he thought. They hadn't given Frank and Zoe any of their story. He looked at Renae and she tried to give him a reassuring smile.

"I'll be right back," she said and hopped out of the Terrain and went into the motel office.

Duncan looked at the parking lot that had city police cars, county sheriff's cars, Florida Highway Patrol vehicles, as well as a number of unmarked cars and SUV's that were obviously law enforcement with their tinted windows and extra antennas. There were at least two dozen vehicles parked in front of all the doors of the motel. Three men, two in uniform and one in plainclothes stood outside one of the motel doors smoking cigarettes and bullshitting, not paying any attention to Duncan or the Terrain.

Renae hopped back in the truck after ten minutes and handed Duncan the room key. "He says we got lucky," she said.

Duncan put the truck in 'Drive' and slowly pulled past all of the cop cars. "If this is lucky, I'd hate to see unlucky."

Renae hit his arm playfully. "The manager said these are all police from other jurisdictions to help with Miami Maxima."

"Is it really that big of a deal?" Duncan asked as he looked at the numbers on the motel doors searching for 118.

"I told you it's huge," Zoe said. "Last year there were over forty thousand people. This year will be even bigger and have even better bands."

Duncan slowed as he reached the motel door but all of the spaces in front of it were occupied by police cars. He pulled onto the street and had to go around the corner to find a parking spot on the curb.

II

Croak had been driving slowly by the motel as he saw the beige GMC Terrain move slowly down the motel lot and then exit to the street. He wanted to stop his white Camry and watch to see which room Duncan and his crew went to but Croak had noticed he'd drawn the attention of the three cops standing outside smoking cigarettes. He'd already driven around the block twice waiting for Renae to get done in the office and now on his third pass all three cops were eyeing his vehicle intently.

Croak turned onto the main road away from the motel and found B-Bob's Grocery about a quarter mile away. He pulled into the lot and found a spot where he could see the front of the Manta Ray Motel. He knew that when Duncan left the motel they'd have to get back on the main road. And seeing as they just now got to the motel, he figured it would be awhile before they would be going anywhere.

It had been a long drive from Disney World and Croak had thought he'd be able to get to Duncan and his money when they stopped for gas or food or something, but at both the stops they had made, the opportunity was too risky. If Croak had a gun he figured it would be different, but he'd lost that in Atlanta and hadn't had time to try to locate another one. All he had was a pocket knife, which would do the trick, but the setting would have to be more private.

He figured eventually they'd end up at a motel and then Croak could make his way to their room, and once inside he'd have the situation under control. But of course he never suspected the motel they chose would be swarming with police. There was no way he could make a move on them at this time. Once again, he'd have to sit and wait.

Croak went into B-Bob's and used the restroom, taking a much needed dump, and then bought two bags of food and drinks and ice for his cooler. As her returned to his car it began to rain. The clock on his dash read 6:16 and he figured Duncan and his crew would be in for the night. He leaned back in his seat, adjusting so as not to put any pressure on his sore shoulder, and drifted off to sleep to the pitter patter of the rain on his car.

III

He wasn't sure if it was the sound of thunder or the plane's tires hitting the runway that woke Taggart. Through the raindrop covered window he could see the lights of Miami International reflecting off the wet pavement. It had been a quick flight from Orlando but he'd slept practically the entire way and was feeling refreshed except for the pain in his shoulder.

His agency, along with the help of Florida law enforcement, had tracked the GMC Terrain's license plates using Department of Transportation cameras on the highways, so they were pretty certain the vehicle was in north Miami. Cooperating agencies were now scanning local street and intersection cameras for a hit on the vehicle but so far hadn't hit the mark. Taggart knew it was just a matter of time and he'd find out where they were. And when he did he'd be ready to pounce.

As the commercial airline slowly taxied to the gate, Taggart checked his phone and wasn't surprised to see a couple of nasty texts from Angie. He'd told her he needed to see this one last case through to the end but she bitched and complained that there would always be one more case. Taggart put his phone away thinking that strippers never sent him nasty texts, they were always happy and ready to party. He wondered if he was really ready to give all that up.

Taggart popped a couple of pain pills, leaned his head back and closed his eyes trying to listen to the rain over the murmur of people's voices.

IV

Duncan lifted his head and opened his eyes. The room was dark and he could hear whispering over the sound of the rain outside. He was lying on his back in a queen sized bed with Renae on her back next to him. They were both naked with blankets pulled up to their chins, though when Duncan had first gotten under the covers he had been wearing his boxer briefs. Renae had told him to get rid of them and he wasn't about to argue as she cuddled up to him like a panda bear hugging a bamboo tree.

Two feet on the other side of Renae was a second queen sized bed with Zoe and Frank. They had crashed out to sleep even quicker than Renae and Duncan had. But now as Duncan looked their direction he could see Zoe's body silhouetted through the street light that poured in from the curtained window that wouldn't fully come together.

Duncan watched the smooth curve of her back and ass slowly rising and falling while her hands held and squeezed her tits. One of Frank's hands slid up her abdomen but she whispered something to him and he pulled his hand away and put it behind his head with his other hand. Zoe slid her hands

174

up through her spiky hair as she rode her man like a slow motion bronco. Her body made a prefect side profile silhouette with the light on the other side of her.

Duncan's cock was propping up the blankets as he looked at Zoe's perky nipples and the rhythmic motion of her ass rising and falling. One of her hands slid to her pussy and Frank whispered something to her; she nodded her head and continued moving slowly atop him.

Duncan rolled on his side quietly, his hard cock bumping against Renae's thigh. He slid his hand over her tight tummy and down to the Y of her crotch and slowly petted her up and down beneath the covers. He could feel the tip of his penis leaking pre-cum onto Renae's leg as he gently stroked her pussy while watching Zoe ride her man's cock.

Frank whispered something and Duncan heard Zoe whisper back, "Not yet."

Renae moaned in her sleep and spread her legs slightly, pressing up against Duncan's throbbing hard-on. Her hand touched his chest, abdomen and then his rigid member. "Mmm," she moaned as her fingers wrapped around him. His own fingers had become slick with her juices as he slid them up and down her pussy lips.

"I want to fuck you," Duncan whispered in her ear.

"Mmm-hmm," she moaned delightfully, her eyes still closed.

Duncan sat up, letting the covers fall away from his shoulders as he got on his knees in between Renae's legs. He put his hands on her inner thighs to open her up to him as he brought the tip of his cock to her warm hole. He pressed against her and wiggled his hips and his cock split her pussy lips open and slid smoothly into her.

"Mmm," Renae moaned as Duncan began to fuck her. He looked over at Zoe who was looking at him while she fucked her man. He was pretty sure she was smiling at him as she began to bounce faster atop Frank's cock. Duncan smiled back as he thrust faster in and out of Renae's tight pussy.

"Ah," Zoe said as the silhouette of her ass bounced up and down faster and faster.

"Oh," Renae said as Duncan's cock slid back and forth like a jackhammer.

Frank gasped and whispered frantically.

"Yes," Zoe said, unable to keep it a whisper.

"Oh yes!" Renae cried.

Frank grunted as he jerked his hips up into Zoe and she continued bobbing wildly atop him, her tits bouncing in perfect synchronicity. "Yes, yes," she said.

Duncan's cock felt like a dam had busted and his fluids gushed into Renae as he growled like a wild bear. His hips continued to convulse against Renae's quivering pussy. He watched Zoe lie down atop her man, her head facing Duncan. He did the same over Renae's body and she wrapped her arms around him, hugging him tightly. He lay there smiling and though he couldn't see Zoe's face in the darkness, he was pretty sure she was smiling, too.

V

Croak was smiling, not believing his luck. He'd awakened in the front seat of the Camry at the edge of B-Bob's parking lot. The time on the dashboard read 11:11 but he didn't need to make a wish because his was already coming true. The myriad of cop cars were all leaving the Manta Ray Motel. He didn't have the slightest idea why all of the vehicles were leaving at this time of night, nor did he care. All he cared about was that this was the opportunity he'd been waiting for.

He started the Camry and drove the quarter mile to the motel. Even though he'd seen the nearly two dozen law enforcement vehicles driving away, he found it hard to believe the parking lot was practically empty. Croak didn't pull into the lot which now had only two vehicles in it, a puke green Prius and a poop brown Ford Edge. Instead he drove around the block to make sure Duncan's Terrain was still parked on the street, which it was.

Croak circled back around and parked next to the office door. The rain had stopped but everything had a glossy sheen covering it. A small bell rang over the office door of the Manta Ray Motel as Croak stepped inside. The office wasn't much bigger than a jail cell, which Croak had experienced a time or two. There was a counter with a computer on it and a magazine rack beside the counter that held tourist brochures guaranteeing fun in the Everglades and dinner boat cruises.

"We're all booked up," the motel manager said as he stepped out of a back room. The short, slender man had a bushy black mustache and black hair pulled back in a two inch pony tail. The man had to be pushing nearly seventy years old but refusing to accept it with his dyed hair and the small hoop earring in his left ear.

"I'm looking for some friends of mine," Croak said. "They checked in earlier this evening. I forgot what room they said they were in."

"Uh-huh", the old man said, not liking the vibe he got from the guy wearing a poncho in Miami. "What was the name?"

"I'm not sure."

"You don't know your friend's name?"

"I know their names," Croak said getting angry. He slipped his hand into his pants pocket and wrapped his fingers around the cold metal of his folding pocket knife. "The room is either under Duncan Koch or Renae Savoy."

"Uh-huh," the motel manager said. He tapped onto the computer keyboard in front of him. "Yes, she checked in earlier. It's a little late, would you like me to ring their room?"

"They're expecting me. If you could just tell me their room number."

"Sorry, son, I can't do that."

"Son?"

"Huh?"

"Are you implying that you're my daddy?"

The old man looked confused and he didn't like the dreadlocked man's tone of voice. He reached for the golf club he kept leaning against the counter by the back doorway. "What are you talking about, son?" he asked as his fingers gripped the five iron.

Croak's right hand struck like a King Cobra, the knife in his hand flicking open as it shot forward and the four inch blade driving through the bridge of the old man's nose and piercing his brain. "I hated my daddy," Croak said as the old man fell convulsing to the floor. The knife was still in Croak's hand, blood droplets falling from the blade onto computer keyboard.

Croak turned the computer screen so that he could see it. Renae Savoy, Room 118, booked for three nights.

VI

"What are you doing?" Renae asked. "I got the room for three nights." She was looking at Duncan in the bathroom mirror as she finished final touches on her make-up. She was wearing a silver shimmering dress that hugged her every curve and barely reached her thighs; if she bent over and touched her toes he was certain he'd see everything underneath.

Duncan glanced over at Zoe and Frank standing by one of the motel beds and then stepped closer to Renae and lowered his voice. "I'm not going to leave it in the room." He was holding the duffel bag that contained the counterfeit money.

"Duncan, it will be fine here. The place is swarming with cops."

"They all left, remember. And I'm not going to trust three quarter of a million dollars to some flimsy motel door."

"Seriously?" Renae hissed and slammed her eyeliner on the counter. "So, what, you're just going to carry around that stupid bag all night?"

"We're going to step outside for a smoke," Zoe said as she and Frank left the room, Neither Duncan nor Renae responded.

Duncan shrugged his shoulders. "Sure, why not? At least I know it's safe."

"That money has been nothing but trouble," Renae said.

"Oh really? It's bought you everything you wanted," Duncan said looking around the room at suitcases filled with goodies from their shopping sprees in Dallas and Atlanta.

"It's gotten people killed. I wish you never had that money."

Duncan laughed. "Right. If I didn't have this money you wouldn't have anything to do with me."

"That's not true."

"What, you would have come to my motel room in the desert and fucked me for free?"

"You're an asshole!" Renae said and slammed the bathroom door in Duncan's face.

The motel door opened and Frank stuck his head in the room and said, "Our ride's here. We've got to go if we're going to make it by midnight"

VII

Where the fuck could they be going at twenty minutes to midnight, Croak wondered. After he'd wiped the blade of his pocket knife clean using the pants leg of the dead motel clerk, he'd quickly checked behind the counter and in the back office in hopes of finding a firearm, but no luck. As he returned to the front office he saw the Buick Enclave pulling into the parking lot and Croak had a moment of panic and grabbed the dead guy and began to pull him into the back.

The SUV didn't stop at the office but instead pulled up alongside the motel door at the far end of the lot. Croak looked through the office window and saw the Buick stopping next to the two teenagers smoking outside. He assumed it was a pizza delivery, which made his stomach grumble. He could definitely use some pizza after he took care of business.

The driver of the SUV didn't get out. There was no pizza and instead the two teenagers were getting into the back of the grey vehicle and a minute later Duncan and Renae exited the motel room looking all snazzy. He noticed Duncan carrying a leather duffel bag.

Croak contemplated waiting till they all left and then going to the motel room and seeing if his money was in there. While searching the back office he'd found the master key for all the motel doors, so getting in would be no problem. The only problem, as Croak saw it, was that he didn't just want the money, he wanted Duncan's head. And he also had a stinking suspicion that the bag Duncan carried might have his money in it.

Croak hopped in his Camry and followed the Enclave. He figured he'd see if the opportunity to take Duncan out presented itself and then he could always come back and check the room if he needed to. And worst case scenario, if he lost Duncan, Croak could simply return to the Manta Ray Motel and be waiting for Duncan in his room.

VIII

Taggart didn't like waiting in his hotel room not far from the airport. After he'd landed he checked in at the U.S. Treasury's branch office where he met with Special Agent in Charge Candy Rose. Taggart was pretty certain he'd met a stripper before with that name, and if not, he knew for certain he'd met more than one Candy and Rose. SAC Candy Rose was definitely no stripper with her squarish body and pail shaped head.

Agent Rose was cordial and professional and explained to Taggart that most of Florida's law enforcement officers were doing overtime working security detail at Miami Maxima which officially began at midnight. She gave Taggart a police radio and said that they still hadn't had any positive ID's of the suspects or their vehicle.

Now as it neared midnight, Taggart was relaxing on the hotel's double bed with his shoes kicked off. On the hotel's movie channel he was watching Hairy Squatter and the Gold Filled Goblet, a porn that had some chick with a 70's bush peeing into a large cup. Taggart wasn't getting into it and he kept the volume low as he listened to the police radio which was mostly quiet.

IX

It was uncomfortably quiet as they rode in the Uber vehicle from the motel towards downtown where half a dozen city blocks would be cordoned off for the multitude of people partying at Miami Maxima. Their driver looked like a forty year old high school teacher but when Frank had tried to engage him in conversation he was polite but curt.

Zoe had tried to engage Renae sitting next to her in the third row of seats; Duncan and Frank were in the second row. "I love those heels," she said as she looked at Renae's silver Pradas that complemented her dress.

"Thanks," Renae said, giving her a brief smile and then returning her attention back out the window.

"I could never wear them," Zoe said. "I suck in heels."

"I like when you suck," Frank laughed.

"Shut up," Zoe said playfully hitting him in the back of the head. Then to Renae she asked, "How do you even learn to be graceful in them?"

"Practice," Renae replied. "They're vital if you're going to be in the profession."

Zoe was wearing a black mini skirt Renae had given her as well as a red blouse that was stretched to the limits with her breasts. She had only the bottom two buttons buttoned and the rest of the shirt open revealing a black bra and lots of skin and cleavage. Renae had offered her heels as well - she had at least two dozen new pairs in the motel room - but Zoe had opted to keep her black flats because she said she'd be dancing all night long.

Duncan had on a black suit with a black shirt and before getting mad at him, Renae had told him he looked cooler than James Bond. Frank was wearing his jeans, tennis shoes and a yellow t-shirt that read 'Warning: Slippery When Wet.' Duncan had offered him another shirt but Frank said he was cool.

"This is so cool," Zoe said as she saw the streets filled with people all walking in the same direction toward downtown. The Uber was in a line of cars that had come to a crawl and people were walking faster than the vehicles were moving.

"This is as close as I can get," the driver said. "Sorry." He stopped the vehicle on the corner and everyone got out. Duncan handed him a hundred dollar bill. "I don't have change for this. The most I--"

"Keep it," Duncan said and shut the door. He thought the driver might have said thanks, but he wasn't paying attention. He grabbed Renae's arm gently and she stopped and turned to him. Zoe and Frank were holding hands and they both stopped and looked back. "Go ahead," Duncan told them, "we'll catch up in a minute."

Frank gave a wave of his hand and he and his girl blended in with the river of excited, flowing people. Cars were honking, people yelling and laughing and jumping around, everybody in a festive mood for what had become one of Miami's most festive outdoor music concerts.

"I'm sorry," Duncan said. He'd moved his hand from her arm to her shoulder as he looked into her eyes. He lifted up the duffel bag in his hand and said, "This money is making me crazy. I'm sorry for all the trouble it's caused us. And I'm sorry about your roommate."

Renae looked down at the ground. The river of people flowed around them on the corner, every now and then someone jostling their shoulders. Duncan kept a firm grip on the bag. "After this weekend," Renae said without looking at him, "I need to go home."

Duncan's hand felt numb on her shoulder. "For good?" he asked.

Slowly she raised her head and looked into his eyes. "I don't know."

Duncan swallowed down the emotion rising up in his chest. He tried to give her shoulder a reassuring squeeze. "Well then let's make it a weekend to remember, okay?"

Renae fought back the tears but didn't trust herself to speak. She nodded her head and tried to smile. Duncan smiled back, just as hard and painful and then put his arm around Renae's shoulders and they joined the flow of people. Two blocks later they caught up with Zoe and Frank who were stopped behind a crowd still a block away from the event.

"What's the hold up?" Duncan asked.

"The same old shit," Frank said. "They've got to check everyone's bags and make sure no one's wearing a suicide vest or packing a machine gun."

Duncan and Renae immediately looked at each other. In the distance loud techno music started up and everyone began to cheer and jump up and down. Duncan and Renae seemed like the only two still figures in the entire mob.

"You could go with them," Duncan said to Renae.

"What would you do?" she asked.

"I don't know, maybe find a bar or something. This is really their thing anyway," he said motioning to Zoe and Frank. "Look at all these people, I'm practically the oldest person here."

Renee looked around the crowd who seemed to be mostly around drinking age, give or take a year or two. "You are definitely a dinosaur here."

"Hey," Duncan said playfully, "I've got a dinosaur bone for you."

"I bet you do, Dino," she said as she rubbed her hip against his crotch. "Hey, what about there," Renae said pointing up at a balcony bar about ten floors up and overlooking the event area. "The entrance looks to be outside their barricades."

They told Zoe and Frank their plan. The two teens said they were going into the event area so they could get so close to the music it vibrated their DNA. Duncan made sure they had enough cash and reminded them the name of the motel and their room number in case they all couldn't find each other again in the madhouse of a crowd.

Duncan kept his right arm snug around Renae's shoulders and his left arm looped through the two handles of the duffel bag as they pushed their way through the throng of people trying to push through the barricade funnel like cattle off to slaughter. Police were thick at the metal waist high fences as they checked everyone and their belongings going into the event area.

The front of the building Duncan and Renae had made their way to was called The Lucille and had a line of people behind red velvet ropes. Manning the ropes were four large bouncers all dressed in black, one of whom was holding a digital tablet which he was checking as three hot looking model types, all blondes in outfits that could almost be considered lingerie, stood anxiously in front of him. He nodded his head and one of the other bouncers pulled aside the rope and the three young ladies swayed their asses with every step they took up the stairs and into the building. One of the ladies was carrying a white purse nearly as big as Duncan's duffel bag and no one had asked to search it.

"At least they're not checking bags," Duncan said. "But look at that line, it'll be hours before we get let in."

"Hardly," Renae said. She looked inside her black and silver Bebe clutch and then shut it. "Do you have any hundreds?" she asked Duncan.

He smiled and looked at the duffel bag hanging at his side. "I've got a few thousand or so. How many do you need?"

"Just five."

"You're going to give the bouncer five hundred dollars?' Duncan asked incredulously.

"Do you want to get in or not? You've got thousands of them, it's not like you're going to miss five, right?"

An argument came to mind against that logic, but he pushed his accountant self into a closet in his mind and shut the door. All he wanted to do was have fun this last weekend with Renae. He knew there was a very good chance he'd never see her again.

X

Undercover Miami Vice officer Joseph Lagenfeldt was certain he'd seen her before. He was positioned inside the large foyer at The Lucille where more than twenty people waited for the elevator doors to open so they could ride to the twelfth floor where the nightclub called Queen was throwing its big bash overlooking the Miami Maxima event area. He'd been standing around in the foyer for almost two hours, always blending with the crowd as if he, too, were waiting for the antique elevator that had an arrow above the doors that moved in an arc showing what floor it was currently on. Once the doors opened and people got on he'd slowly drift off to the side and let the doors close while he remained in the foyer awaiting the next batch of partiers.

Lagenfeldt was good with faces and he'd recognized more than a couple big time drug dealers and a few high class call girls moving among the groups getting on the elevator. At first he took the sexy blonde with the dark roots in the three thousand dollar dress and two thousand dollar heels to be another hooker. But he couldn't place her and that bugged him because he never forgot a face. She was hanging on a man who was dressed nice but his features were soft and his hair cut like a square, not someone who hung out with thousand dollar an hour call girls. Yet something was familiar about him, too.

The elevator bell dinged, the doors opened and the crowd of twenty parted as three people exited the elevator and then everyone but Lagenfeldt got on. The elevator doors closed

185

and the arrow above the door slowly moved in an arc marking each floor as it passed until it stopped on number twelve. There were still five more floors above the one which the nightclub was on.

"Sonofabitch!" the undercover officer said to himself. "I knew it!" He was holding his phone and looking at a BOLO memo.

People were beginning to fill the foyer and Lagenfeldt turned his back on them and walked to a corner away from everyone. He discretely pulled his police radio from his coat pocket and said, "I've got a possible ID on two wanted suspects, file two-three-dash-seven-one-five. Please advise."

While he was on the radio he didn't see the man in the poncho slip out of the group waiting for the elevator and push through the doorway to the stairs.

Ten minutes later two uniformed Miami police officers had joined undercover officer Lagenfeldt near the elevator and the bouncers outside had been informed not to let anyone else into the foyer.

"Whoa, hold up!" Lagenfeldt said to the bald man rushing into the building. "This area is off limits." One of the uniformed officers had his hand on his sidearm.

"Special Agent Taggart, I heard the call," he said as he flashed his badge.

"We've secured the area and are awaiting SWAT," the undercover cop said. "These suspects have shot at federal agents."

"Yeah, I'm that agent," Taggart said, choosing not to correct him that Duncan and Renae had never actually shot at anyone. But sometimes Be On Look Out's had to be worded to catch people's attention. "I'm going up," Taggart said and pressed the elevator button. The doors opened and he stepped in.

"That's not protocol," Lagenfeldt told him.

"You do your job, I'll do mine." The doors closed and Taggart checked his Glock and stuck it back in his waistband holster.

XI

"Is that a gun in your pocket or are you just happy to see me?" Renae asked as Duncan pressed up behind her.

"Very happy," he said. And he was. He was glad they had gotten over whatever that rough bump was and the tension they'd felt in the car ride over had all dissipated. He just wanted to have fun with Renae, all he'd ever wanted since the moment he'd met her, and he was going to do everything possible to keep things on a fun level, no more fighting or negativity. And now that they were all the way in Miami there should be no more Croak or federal agents following them. They could relax and have fun.

Renae was leaning over the railing and looking down at the street twelve stories below. There was a huge stage and light show on one side of the street and tens of thousands of people jumping and moving to the intensely loud techno and dub step music filling the air. About four blocks down the street was another large stage and a band or DJ playing, Renae couldn't tell which, and more wall to wall people. She wiggled her ass against Duncan's half chub that was rubbing between her ass cheeks.

She stood up straight and spun Duncan around so his back was against the railing and she was in front of him, pressing herself against his hardening member. The rooftop balcony was almost as crowded as the street below and loud, deafening music was blaring from speakers on the club walls. Renae leaned into him, her tits squashing against his chest, and put her mouth to his ear. "What if you fucked me right here against the railing, do you think anyone would even know?"

Renae slipped her tongue into Duncan's ear and shoved her hand down the front of his pants to grab his thick, rock hard, velvety cock. "Or maybe we should find a bathroom stall," she breathed into his wet ear.

Duncan's hands went to her ass as his mouth found her's and he kissed her passionately. She squeezed his cock as their tongues swirled. His fingertips slipped under the hem of her short dress and touched the warm, bare flesh of her ass. He let one of his fingers slide to her ass crack and her hand began jerking him off, sliding up and down the tight, veiny flesh of his stiff rod. His mouth devoured her and she sucked on his tongue while he squeezed her ass and she squeezed his cock and their bodies pressed up tight against one another. He wanted to fuck her so bad but he couldn't move. He was lost in her kiss, her touch, her essence. He could explode right here into her hand in his pants but that wasn't good enough. He wanted to be in her. He needed to be in her.

"Come on," he said, grabbing her hand out of his pants and pulling her through the thick crowd. If anyone had seen what they had been doing, Duncan didn't know and didn't care. All he cared about was the woman holding onto his hand. He looked across the bar for a sign designating the bathrooms. What he saw almost made him go to the bathroom in his pants.

XII

"Holy shit!" Duncan cried. "I think that's the cop."

"What cop? Where?"

"Get down!" he said and pulled Renae down in a crouch and they pushed through the crowd until they were behind some planters on the balcony. Duncan pointed across the crowd. "I don't know if that's him or not."

"He's definitely looking for somebody."

"Shit, if that's who I think it is, he's a fucking Treasury agent." Duncan held up his duffel bag waist high for emphasis.

Renae started laughing.

"It's not funny. Why are you laughing?"

"I don't know," she said with tears in her eyes. "It's all just so crazy."

"It looks like he's going to the bathrooms," Renae said. The bathrooms they could see now were located on the other side of the elevator.

"Let's get out of here," Duncan said and he and Renae moved as quickly as they could through the crowd. There were half a dozen people directly in front of the elevator, a couple of them looking up at the arrow that was moving from 11 to 12. As Duncan and Renae got closer, the elevator dinged, the doors opened and two Miami police officers stepped out. Duncan jerked Renae through a door that read: 'Stairway' but he feared it didn't lead to heaven.

XIII

What the hell, Taggart thought after checking the bathroom. He knew they had to be up here somewhere. It was possible the cop downstairs could have been mistaken in his ID, but Taggart didn't think so. He had a hunch they were somewhere close.

He exited the bathroom and saw the two cops standing in front of the elevator talking to a black clad bodybuilder that Taggart took for club security. It was the same two police officers from downstairs.

"Is there any other way out of here?" Taggart asked the bouncer.

"Just the stairs," the big man said pointing to the doorway fifteen feet away. "But after hours all the doors are locked. Once you go through you can't come back; only the ground floor door will open."

Taggart asked one of the police officers to radio downstairs and make sure someone was watching the stairway door. "No one's come through since you've been up here," the police officer relayed.

"Okay," Taggart said. "Do you know who we're looking for?" The bouncer shook his head as the cops said they got the BOLO. Taggart pulled out his phone and showed the bouncer the pictures of Duncan and Renae. He then told him to check the storerooms and kitchen. Taggart left one of the cops at the elevator and told the other to come with him. They began

189

slowly pushing through the shoulder to shoulder crowd scanning every face, looking for the suspects.

XIV

"Do you think they're really looking for us?" Renae asked.

"I don't know, but it's not a chance I'm willing to take. Let's just go back to the motel," Duncan said as he and Renae began to walk down the stairs. "Zoe and Frank can have their fun here, we'll have our fun back in the room."

"It was certainly fun waking up to you inside me," she replied squeezing his hand. She stopped when they reached the next floor below and said, "Wait!" She bent over.

Duncan looked at her sweet ass, the bottom of her cheeks peeking out beneath the low hemline. His dick that had deflated as they made their escape in the club, began to stir. "We can't do that right now," he told her.

"What? I'm taking off my heels so I don't kill myself going down the stairs." She stood up holding her heels and gave Duncan a peck on the lips. "You perv."

"It's hard not to be with you," he said smiling and then they began moving quicker down the stairs. As they turned the corner in the stairwell just past the seventh floor, Duncan froze. His body felt like someone had just dumped a bucket of ice water over his head.

"What?" Renae asked, looking at Duncan. He let go of her hand and put his sweaty hand to her mouth. Duncan's eyes looked like that of a rat's about to be eaten by a snake. He turned his head back down the stairwell.

Just stepping off the bottom step one flight below them was a man with multicolored dreadlocks hanging almost to his ass over a dirty brown and grey poncho. Renae sucked in her breath and cringed against Duncan and he put his arm around her.

Croak stopped as he was about to round the corner of the stairwell and as if in slow motion his head swiveled over his shoulder and he looked up the stairwell at Duncan and Renae. An evil smile parted his lips. "Hey, buddy," Croak said as an uncle might say to his favorite nephew.

Duncan grabbed Renae's hand and they ran back upstairs. When they reached the seventh floor landing he grabbed the doorknob of the stairwell door but it was locked. "Shit!" he spat and grabbed Renae's hand and they ran up the stairs.

Croak laughed somewhere below and called out, "Where do you think you're going to go?"

They reached the twelfth floor, Duncan breathing hard and his face covered in sweat. Renae was looking down the stairwell as Duncan tried the door. They could hear the throbbing music coming from the other side.

"It's locked," Duncan said.

"Knock on it," Renae said.

Duncan shook his head. "Nobody's going to hear anything over that music." he grabbed her hand again. "Come on!" Up the stairs they went.

"I've got you now, motherfucker!" Croak yelled from below. It sounded like he was a couple flights below them as they reached the fourteenth floor. Duncan hopelessly tried the doorknob but all was locked on fourteen, fifteen, sixteen, seventeen, and eighteen. The stairwell continued up, though a red sign on the wall said: 'Roof Access, Authorized Personnel Only.'

They reached the door to the roof, but it, too, was locked. Duncan slammed his shoulder into the door as he'd seen done in the movies and immediately regretted it. The steel door didn't budge and his shoulder felt like it had been hit with a baseball bat.

Duncan turned his back to the door and slammed his foot against it in a donkey kick. Nothing happened and he kicked it again.

"Here comes the reaper!" Croak yelled from one flight below them.

"Duncan," Renae said worriedly looking at him and then down the empty flight of stairs.

Duncan kicked his foot against the door multiple times and the door flew open.

XV

Duncan fell back through the open doorway, landing onto his ass on the gravel covered rooftop. Renae rushed through the doorway, ignoring the sharp rocks biting into the bottom of her bare feet.

Holding the door open with a key on a chain still stuck in the lock was an elderly Puerto Rican wearing a blue security guard uniform with a silver badge pinned over the left hand pocket. "What are you doing pounding on the goldarn door?" he asked as Renae helped Duncan to his feet.

Duncan ran to the edge of the rooftop and looked around frantically. "Is there another way down?" The sound coming from the street a hundred and eighty feet below was so loud it could have been a rooftop band. The jumping and dancing people looked like little ants climbing all over each other.

"No one is allowed up here," the old man told him. "This is for authorized--"

"Look out!" Renae screamed.

Rather than look behind him the security guard looked at Renae and then his eyes grew wide and he seemed to levitate about a foot off the roof. The man's mouth moved but no sound came out, only bright red blood that ran down his chin.

Croak was behind the security guard, his knife stuck in the old man's lower back. He had lifted the frail man off his feet and was now propelling him toward the edge of the building.

"No!" Renae screamed as Croak pushed the man off the roof of The Lucille. The old man's body slid off of Croak's knife and he fell into the darkness on the opposite side of the building from the Miami Maxima concert. The sound of his body hitting the street below was drowned out by a dub step beat.

Croak turned and pointed his bloody knife at Duncan and said, "You're next."

"Renae, run!" Duncan yelled at her.

She looked at Croak, her tear filled eyes wide, and then she turned toward the open rooftop door.

"Oh no you don't!" Croak yelled and took two leaping bounds toward the terrified woman.

Duncan also ran for her, but he was at the back edge of the building. Croak reached Renae first and looped his left arm around her throat and swung her toward the edge of the roof overlooking the Miami Maxima concert. Croak grimaced through the pain in his shoulder and he brought the tip of his knife up and pointed it at Renae's sternum.

Duncan stopped ten feet away and cried out, "You don't have to do that, Croak!"

"Of course I don't have to," he laughed. "Maybe I want to."

"She didn't do anything, just let her go," Duncan pleaded.

"It's beyond that now," Croak said. "You made me shoot my best friend in the back. So maybe I just throw her off the roof to even the score. Didn't you ever do that with kittens, throw them off the roof just to see how they'd land?"

"No," Duncan said, his eyes locked on Renae. "I also didn't pull the legs off spiders or burn ants with a magnifying glass."

"You had a deprived childhood," Croak said.

"Come on, Croak, I've got the money right here," Duncan said and lifted the duffel bag in his hand.

XVI

"Drop it!" Taggart yelled as he leaned against the door frame on The Lucille rooftop. He had his gun shifting back and forth from Duncan to Croak. Duncan wasn't sure if the agent meant for him to drop his bag or for Croak to drop his knife.

"I'll drop her alright," Croak said, still clinging to Renae in a choke hold. "Right over the edge."

"And then I'll drop you," Taggart said, his gun pointing towards Croak.

"No," Duncan said, "everybody just calm down." Renae's eyes were on Duncan as her hands clung to Croak's forearm pressing against her throat. She was finding it difficult to breathe and her legs were feeling weak.

"There's no way you're getting away, Allyn," Taggart said. "Cops are everywhere."

Anger washed over Croak's face as he said, "My fucking dad called me Allyn and he's dead. My name is Croak."

"I don't care if your name is Ass Munch, you're not getting out of here."

"Watch me," Croak growled and he brought the edge of the blade to Renae's cheek and made a small slice. Renae screamed but she was feeling too weak to struggle in his arm as blood made a line down her cheek and dripped from her chin.

"Stop, stop, stop!" Duncan screamed. He turned to Taggart and said, "If he's not getting out of here, then just put the gun down. What have you got to lose?"

"The next time the blade takes out an eye," Croak said as he held the blade tip of his knife near Renae's eye socket.

"Please?" Duncan begged.

"Okay, fine," Taggart scowled and slowly set his gun on the gravel roof in front of him.

"Kick it over here," Croak told him.

"You're not getting the gun," Taggart said and instead kicked it a few feet to the side of him, away from Croak.

Duncan feared this would further anger Croak so he held up the bag of money. "I've got your money right here."

"Hand it over," Croak demanded.

"Let her go first."

"Stop trying to be a tough guy," Croak told Duncan, "it's not you." Renae was practically limp in his grasp and he dangled one of her feet over the edge of the building.

Taggart glanced toward his Glock, pretty sure he could get to it in one leap.

Croak read the agent's intentions and said, "Do it and I drop her!"

"Here!" Duncan yelled, handing the duffel bag toward Croak.

Croak grabbed one of the handles of the bag with his hand still holding the knife. "Let go!" Croak said, his eyes watching to make sure the agent hadn't made a move.

"Give me your hand," Duncan said to Renae. Her eyes were closed and she opened them slowly. "Your hand!" Duncan yelled at her. She slowly raised her right arm. Then Croak pushed her off the roof.

XVII

Duncan dove for Renae as Taggart dove for his gun. Croak had caught them both by surprise as he yanked the duffel bag free from Duncan and in three long strides he was kicking at Taggart's left wrist that was bringing up the Glock. Though the agent had trained at the range using both hands, he was right hand dominant but after taking the shot in the right shoulder there was no way he could fire with that hand. He was certain if he'd been able to scoop his Glock up in his right hand he would have beaten Croak to the punch and gotten off some shots. As it was, Croak's cowboy boot snapped Taggart's left wrist and the gun went soaring through the air over the edge of the building.

Duncan had gotten his fingers around Renae's right wrist and as she fell over the side of The Lucille her weight threw Duncan hard to the gravel rooftop. Renae's body smacked into the side of the building and then she was dangling almost two hundred feet above the street filled with fifty thousand party goers.

"Renae, you're slipping!" Duncan yelled. "Grab onto me with your other hand. Renae!" She was unresponsive.

Croak kept his momentum moving forward after kicking the agent and he made it to the threshold of the roof doorway when he was being yanked off his feet and slammed to the rooftop hard on his back. Taggart had managed to snag a couple fistfuls of the long dreadlocks and jerked on them like he was pulling on a dog's leash. Taggart leaped onto the man's right arm, knowing he needed to contain the knife that it held. The leather duffel bag had dropped a couple feet away from the two men.

Duncan could feel Renae slipping through his fingers. His legs and other arm were spread out like a flat tripod on the roof to keep from being pulled over the side. There was no way he could reach her with his left hand and if he tried to regrip her wrist with his right hand she would fall to her death. "Renae! Please! I can't lose you. Renae!" She was slipping.

Duncan felt like he was in a tunnel or falling down a rabbit hole. The sounds of the music on the street below and all of the people yelling and clapping and stomping their feet began to fade away and a heavy wind picked up blowing Duncan's hair wildly and swinging Renae's body against the building.

"This is the police!" a loudspeaker blared and then a bright light was illuminating Duncan and Renae as a SWAT team helicopter came from around the side of the building and hovered fifty feet away in the air. "You're under arrest. Don't move!" announced the loudspeaker.

But Renae was moving, her wrist sliding from Duncan's sweaty fingers and all he could think was that he should have gone to the gym more. Over the sound of the helicopter rotors

Duncan could still hear the heavy beat of the music on the street and he was sure the partygoers had to be looking up at the spectacle above them. He wondered if from eighteen floors below they could tell that Renae wasn't wearing any panties under her silver dress. And then we wondered why in the hell he was wondering that at a time like this and as her wrist lost contact with his fingers he realized she was right, he was a perv.

Duncan hadn't realized he'd closed his eyes due to the strong wind created by the helicopter rotors but he opened them quickly when he felt the small hand clasping to his wrist. Renae was clinging to him with her other hand; the blustery wind and roar of the helicopter and awakened her. Duncan quickly clamped his fingers around her wrist and then her other hand locked onto his arm. "Come on, baby, you can do it!" he yelled as he pulled and she climbed. Tears streamed down his face as he cried, "I've got you!"

XVIII

"I've got you!" Taggart said as he banged Croak's knife hand against the rooftop gravel. Croak ignored the pain as he brought his left hand as hard as he could into the agent's groin. It was with his bad shoulder, though it had been a week since he'd been shot; but then it doesn't take a lot to crush a man's balls.

Taggart doubled over and rolled off of Croak. Croak rolled on top of Taggart and slashed downward at the agent's face with his pocket knife, still bloody from Renae, the security guard and traces of the motel manager. Taggart moved his head at the last fraction of a second and the knife blade sparked against the gravel. Croak brought the knife back up and tried to jab it into Taggart's throat.

Taggart got his hands up to intercept Croak's wrist but he couldn't hold him. Taggart's right shoulder screamed with pain and his left wrist felt like the broken bones were being grinded against broken glass. Bloody spittle drooled from Croak's evil grin as he pushed down on the knife towards Taggart's throat, the agent's resistance weakening.

"I hated my daddy!" Croak growled and Taggart had no idea what that meant and feared he never would. The knife came down as his arms gave out and then Croak was violently flung off the top of him while Taggart was bathed in a bright light from above.

The SWAT team helicopter light followed the action as Duncan swung the leather duffel bag and knocked the dreadlocked man off of the bald guy. When Duncan had bashed the bag into Croak the zipper had burst open and a handful of hundreds flew out of the bag. The rotor wash from the helicopter sent the bills swirling in the air.

Croak was quickly on his feet and he lunged at Duncan with his knife. Duncan jumped back and swung the duffel bag at Croak. More hundred dollar bills flew out of the bag and swirled in and out of the circle of light cast by the helicopter's searchlight.

"Stop wasting my fucking money!" Croak roared and charged at Duncan, the knife aiming for his face. Duncan blocked the blow with the leather bag, Croak's knife driving into it as he rushed forward. The bag burst open. Duncan fell to his side on the rooftop a foot from the edge. Croak's feet tripped over Duncan and the dreadlocked maniac in the poncho went over the side of the building.

The leather duffel bag sprayed thousands of hundred dollar bills into the air which fluttered wildly beneath the overhead helicopter. The partygoers eighteen stories below turned into a shark frenzy as everyone scrambled for the raining money.

Renae rushed to Duncan's side and collapsed crying in his arms. Taggart sat up slowly as SWAT officers rushed onto the roof from the stairwell. Never a cop when you need one, Taggart thought.

Part 14

Worth It

Duncan stood on the fly bridge of his forty-seven-foot yacht in the small marina up the coast from Miami. He was watching a bright yellow vintage Corvette that had pulled into the parking lot fifty yards away. The tall, slender blonde that got out of the car moved with the grace and confidence of a supermodel. The white shorts she wore emphasized her tan legs that ended in yellow and white heels that probably cost more than most suburbanites' rent. She wore an unbuttoned white blouse that was tied into a knot beneath her breasts, which were encased in a light yellow bikini top.

"I didn't figure you for a vintage car kind of girl," Duncan said when she stopped beside the yacht.

She removed her Versace sunglasses and looked up at him. "It was Stacy's. I couldn't sell it."

"You look good in it."

"You look pretty good in your new ride, too," Renae said. "Permission to come aboard?"

Duncan came down from the fly bridge and then held out a hand as he helped Renae onto the yacht. "Did you see the name?" he asked her.

"Fantasia's Fantasy," she said and smiled. "But this was your fantasy, not mine."

"Yeah, but 'Duncan's Fantasy' didn't have the same ring to it." He offered her a seat and got them drinks before sitting next to her.

"How much trouble did you get into?" Duncan asked.

Renae took a sip of her drink. "Mmm. None really. Kiki and I had to give statements about the money that had been paid to us that we didn't know was counterfeit, and how she was kidnapped and you and I had tried to save her. You know they're watching you, right?"

"Yeah, I know. But how do you know?"

"Agent Taggart and I talk sometimes."

"Oh really?"

"He had a thing for my roommate."

"I'm sure that's not all he's got a thing for."

"You're such a perv." Renae took another drink. "He knows you saved his life on the rooftop and he's not after you, just so you know. He's actually leaving the agency and moving to Ohio with his wife."

"Good for him."

"He said he couldn't figure out how you had money to buy this boat if it all scattered off the roof that night."

"I'm an accountant. Accountants know how to squirrel away money. Sometimes it's in banks and sometimes it's in the spare tire wheel well of an SUV."

Renae smiled. "You're not worried they could track the funny money?"

Duncan shook his head. "Not when there's been half a million floating around the past few months."

"I thought there was almost eight hundred thousand?"

Duncan smiled.

"You kept three hundred thousand?"

Duncan kept smiling.

"Did you spend it all on this boat?"

"It's not a boat, it's a yacht," Duncan said and finished his drink. "What's with all the questions? How do I know you're not a cop?"

Renae finished her drink and set the glass next to Duncan's. "Do you want to taste me and see?"

"I think I'd better," he said as he stood up and took her hand, leading her into the master stateroom.

"I've never done it on a boat before," Renae said from inside the yacht.

"Me neither," Duncan replied.

"What? It's been over three months. What have you been doing?"

"Waiting for you."

THE END

About the Author

D. Mann has spent half his adult life in state and federal prisons and the other half in strip clubs, casinos and dark places. He has gone by many names and draws his stories from a lifetime of unconventional adventure.

Deviant Ways Publications
PO Box 94 – Montrose, MN 55363